one Hot winter in Estes

For Kathy & Fred

— Enjoy!

a novel by
Randy St.John

Randy St Johns

Published by
Pigiron Productions, Inc.
PO Box 321
Estes Park, Colorado, 80517
(970) 586-0638

I was going to dedicate this Novel to my Mother, who taught me to love writing. Then I wanted to dedicate it to my brother Ted, who taught me to read. Realistically, though, it is for my brother Mick and his wife Nancy who lent me the money to make rent while I finished writing this puppy.

*   *   *   *   *

This book is a work of fiction.
The Town of Estes Park has been my home for over a decade. It has been home to the Wheel Bar since 1945, Marlin has been the bartender there since Pontius was a Pilot, and Delmar's is the best place in town to buy a six-pack and a bottle. Aside from that, any semblance of the characters found within these pages to any person living or dead is purely coincidental. Some of the buildings named in the town exist, but not as depicted in my writings. We have a Town Council, a Mayor, and a Chief of Police. They are honest and honorable people and the Offices of these Ladies and Gentlemen were portrayed how they were portrayed for the sake of this story, this tale, this work of fiction. Don't take the words of this book seriously but, rather, enjoy the foolish imagination of the man who wrote a make-believe yarn. The six acts of terrorism occurring within this book have certainly been perpetrated, but not all by the Author and never in Estes Park. Have as much fun reading this narrative as I had writing it, but never forget that it is only a fable!

January, 1996
Estes Park, Colorado

Library of Congress Catalog Number 94-12045
ISBN 0-9650328-0-9
Copyright © 1996 by PIGIRON Productions, Inc.

Second Printing   February 1998

Chapter One

I don't really like people very much, but as a waiter I don't have to like people very much. As a waiter I can't be sure whether or not I like you until after you leave anyway, but you don't need to know that. You only need to think that I like you, and you only need to think that until you leave, but that doesn't mean I need to be rude. This is a tourist town and I'll probably never see you again, but I take pride in what I do and I like what I do and whatever I think of you has little to do with what I think of my job. Likewise, what you think of me should have little to do with how you enjoy your meal. So long as the food is good and on time and I'm as courteous as I can be, you shouldn't have any complaints. I don't know why some people want to be openly rude, but some do, and that irritates me. In the Kitchen making a salad or filling a canoli the other waiters and I compare notes as to who has the most clueless table in the restaurant, and that makes us laugh and relives the tension. It does nothing, however, to relieve fear. I have never felt fear as a waiter, and I wouldn't know how to deal with it except for how I would otherwise deal with fear: Face it square-on and hope it doesn't show because I'm not a physically intimidating person and I have only my wits to carry me through.

I noticed that the guy on Table Four was carrying a gun when he sat down, but guns don't bother me and I had no intention of pissing him off that bad so I didn't do much other than notice it then forget it. Maybe somebody with a gun in an Italian restaurant in New York City might be cause for concern, but not in some back-woods burg in The Rockies. He had been acting a little anxious when he sat down, but a lot of people are that way before dinner only to become the model of civility once they'd crammed a couple pounds of carbohydrates down their gut, and I had no reason to believe this one would be any different. Yes, I did have a reason, because he'd had more than a couple Bourbons and kept getting more surly every time I got near. He was not enjoying the company of the two men he was with and they were reciprocating in kind, and with the Dining Room almost deserted at this hour his raspy voice was becoming a little too loud and curt in the gestures he was making for me to be very relaxed around the table. You could say that I was openly avoiding them but I could say that I was simply doing the side-work I always do before we close. His coat was open and the gun was almost blatant in its' presence, and when he turned in his chair, slammed his meaty fist on the table, and rasped "Waiter!" across the room there was no more pretending that his mood would change for the better or that I would be charming him into being the gentleman he wasn't. It wasn't my fault that he had been punched in the throat so many times he sounded like an old John Deere, but I didn't feel at all like discussing it with him. As I headed toward the door next to me and called back, "be right there", his "you'd better be" bit the back of my neck hard enough to push me the last few steps out of the Dining Room and into the Kitchen.

The Kitchen. Quiet now at the end of the night, so clean and white and familiar. The place where all the nice things are made and the jokes are told and we Waitrons can laugh at the Dinning Room antics. They can't find us in the Kitchen. The law says they can't come in here. This is our place alone, and I'm feeling very alone right now. Where is the law when some burly, gun-toting thug is half-in-the-bag thirty feet away and he's not angry with the food or the music or our beautiful Kitchen but he's angry nonetheless and he's looking for me? I've faced angry people with guns before, but then I was in a Military Uniform and twenty years younger and had a gun of my own. This is different, very different and very alone, and I have nowhere to go but back out into the Dining Room. Just loop to the Dinning Room through the Lounge and come up from another direction, which may not make any difference to him but I'll feel better about it because there are a few people in the Lounge still working on a last cocktail. A last cocktail sounds almost absurd right now, because is it a last cocktail before you go home to a loving family or to a nagging spouse or just a last cocktail in general? Ten steps though to the bar to where the bottles are all standing like tall clean sentinels of good cheer. "Be of good cheer" they clamor, smiling absurdly through their white and black and amber faces. "Be of good cheer", as they usher me on my way. Two more steps to the station where so many times I have called for

2

an order. Call for an order now; any sort of order, like a Scotch-and-Soda or a Budweiser or an order to life and the circumstances surrounding it that seem suddenly out of control. "Order please. Please let there be order!" The order comes, okay, and it's an order to keep walking past where the light from the wine rack is always too bright for the people on Table Four because it shines into their eyes, and his eyes were squinting at me as I came into his view and his lips were drawn and his lapel was bulged unnaturally from what was under it. He couldn't see my eyes because the light was now behind them, and that was good because they would have told him what I didn't want him to know.

"Boy", he started, and I think I started too, because that's just how I felt.

"Boy, since there's nobody in here now but us, there's something I want to ask you."

I didn't try to answer because he had my attention and he knew he had my attention and I don't know if I could have said anything just then anyhow.

"Boy, do you think it would be okay if we smoked in here since we're all alone?"

"It's always been okay to smoke in here", I choked. "There should have been an ashtray on the table when you sat down. Let me find one for you."

The three cigarettes were already lit in the time it took me to turn, grab an ashtray from the shelf, turn again, and put it on the table.

"You know" he reminisced to the other two as he casually rolled the tip of his smoke in the ashtray, "the Force is going the way of the Military and it just doesn't make any sense to me. They only want to hire men who don't smoke because they think smoking looks bad. They give you a God-damned gun and a baton and 'cuffs and tell you to wear them in plain sight outside of a uniform that was designed to be intimidating, but they don't want you to smoke because they think it may tarnish the image behind that shiny badge. Maybe I'll take that early retirement after all. Tell me, boy, you ever think about retirement?"

3

"Yeah, I got to thinking about that seriously two minutes ago, and if it's all the same to you I'd just as soon not do that again for a few years".

"Don't play me, boy, I'm asking you a question and I want an answer. You ever think about retirement or do you expect to step-and-fetch-it for the rest of your life?

"I tell you what. You have an ashtray and I have a job and why don't we both fill them as best we can? May I refresh your drink or are you all okay for now because I have things to do?

"You don't have to get smart with me, boy. Yeah, I'm ready for another Black Jack/Rocks, and when you bring that, bring another chair. You don't have that much to do and a customer wants to talk with you for a minute. Do you think you can do that?

"Sure, I can do that for a minute. You other gentlemen care for a refill too?" What an exit line. Here I am getting more booze for somebody who two minutes ago I thought was going to kill me. Coming down from an adrenalin rush, or maybe the way hostages develop a relationship with their captors, I don't know, but I told him I'd sit down for a minute and now I'm looking forward to it. So why does that inspire some sense of relief? Relief would be for these guys to just leave after tipping me heavily, or relief would be for these guys to have never come in the first place. Can you feel relief after an event that never occurred? We probably do it every day and just don't realize it, like almost being in the right place at the right time, and I've got this strange sense of it right now and it's making me feel somewhere between a little bit brave and almost pissed-off.

"Gentlemen, here are your drinks, here is a chair, and here am I, but unless you knock-off calling me "boy" two of those items are going to go away. I've mentioned twice since you sat down that my name is Jimmy and you ought to try using it. I like it, I respond well to it, and ..."

"Okay, Jimmy-Boy, sit down and relax. I'm not trying to piss you off, but enough people have already pissed me off today that you get what's left over. Is that your shift drink?"

"He lets us have one. It may be a little early, but he's gone home and I'm almost done anyway so it doesn't matter."

"You always drink behind the boss's back?"

4

"I'm not doing anything behind the boss's back", I muttered into his eyes, getting out of the chair. I'd had about enough of his bullying tactics and my tolerance for Chicken-Shit hadn't gotten any greater than it was when I got out of the Navy half a life-time ago. "If you'll excuse me, I have some cleaning to do so I can get out of here". By the time I got to the Kitchen which had a few minutes ago been so comforting I was worked into a frame of mind that wouldn't have found comfort at my mother's breast. Some people can have that reaction with me, and it's one of the reasons that I think it's time I make a career change. Not that I don't still get a kick in the pants out of waiting tables. I think it's probably the best job I've ever had, but people like that pompous ass in the dining room are beginning to get to me a little too often these days, and that isn't a good sign. Most of the jobs I've ever had have ended without a good sign. What sort of sign is making sure I get all of the spots off the glass doors of the reach-in refrigerator? ("Gee, Daddy what did you do in the war?" "I cleaned the glass, dear, and I did it very well.") "I really should get a job", I said to myself.

"Maybe I got one for you if your not going to run away and pout every time things ain't going your way."

Nothing like a raspy voice to get your attention when you lose yourself in your thoughts, but at least he'd taken the time to button his jacket. And he was smiling, which made me skeptical but at least relaxed enough to be willing to listen to him. It is amazing the perspective to life a clean sheet of glass will give if you look at it long and hard enough, and my life had just taken one of those mini-revelations which satisfy for the moment even if they don't last longer than that. A fleeting glimpse of clarity, for lack of a better expression.

"You ready for another drink? Mike should be at the bar, unless you want me to step-and-fetch-it for you."

"No I don't want another drink. You should warn people about the effect this altitude has on alcohol."

"Elevation. Altitude is what you gain after you drink at this elevation, and I usually do warn people about it. I might have said something to you too, but you never gave me the chance. You need me for anything? I don't play in the cash register, so you'll need somebody else if you're leaving. If you're looking for a friend, you left two of them in the other room."

"We're leaving, but not quite yet. Look, Jimmy, I don't make friends very easy, but that's my fault and I don't make much of an effort to change because friends aren't that important to me. I don't want you to be my friend. What I do want is to make an offer to you and I think you'll want to hear it."

Standing eye-ball to eye-ball with him for the first time I realized I had about four or five inches on him. It made me wonder if he was the stereotypically undesirable cop; the undersized kid who got beat up on his way home from school every day and subjugated that frustration in adulthood by becoming the bully he had feared. Probably, but it didn't matter. He had an offer for me and I wanted to hear it just to change the subject. Why was it that every time I tried to talk to this guy I found that the first thing I wanted to do was change the subject?

"Go for it. I'm listening, if you don't mind that I clean the kitchen behind my boss's back."

"Okay, I deserved that. The deal is, you've lived in Estes Park long enough to be anonymous. I want you to do something I can't do, and I'm willing to cut you in on a fair share. A simple bit of crawling around under a building or two. I can't do it and I wouldn't let the clowns with me in on it. How does it sound so far?"

"It sounds like breaking-and-entering to me, and I don't do that. You're right that I'm anonymous, so far as getting lost in a crowd is concerned, but I also belong to the local Antique Car Club and hob-nob with the Banker and the Chief of Police and a few other minor dignitaries in this town who enjoy seeing someone my age who doesn't do drugs and doesn't drink-and-drive and doesn't break-and-enter. I also don't get stopped by the local cops when I do drink-and-drive because they don't expect it of me. I'm happier with that than what ever it is that I expect to hear from you. You're a cop, so why don't you act like one and go get one of those snitches you guys have on the line to do whatever it is you want done? You shouldn't need to recruit raw talent."

"What raw talent? You go by Jimmy, but your name is James Loren and you came to this town ten years ago to visit a friend

6

and do some prospecting. You'd been prospecting in Arizona for over three years and saw Estes Park as a good excuse to avoid another 117° summer. Before that you spent four years in the Navy, were married for the next seven and got a business degree that you never tried to use. Am I close so far?"

"Closer than it's any of your business to be, but I've given the same information to lots of people. What bugs me is that you would want to learn so much about someone else's life in the first place."

"Why would I leave New York City to eat Italian food in Colorado, Jimmy?"

"Maybe because it gave you the chance, any chance, to leave New York City. Maybe you felt the unspoken urge to have a polite waiter who wasn't burned-out on rude people. Why do you want to change the subject again?"

"I didn't come out here just to see you, and I'm not changing the subject. The other guys in the Dinning Room had to pick-up a warrant arrest, but when they got here she was already in some unwittingly stupid jail that won't release her until Monday. I'm their boss so and that gave me the opportunity to take a few days to drive out and watch them do their best, and believe me it's a bitter pill to take. So I didn't come out here just to see you, but it isn't quite the random encounter that it might seem to be."

"What's going on? Since you took the time to find out this much about me you must have stumbled across a note somewhere that mentioned my low tolerance for games."

"You went prospecting about three years out of college and never found squat worth mining, but you read a lot and learned a lot and then came up here. You went to work for The Oliver Hotel as a dishwasher because you wanted a little jingle in your pocket and found gold on the Hotel property but you never told anyone about it except one person. Me, one night at the Wheel Bar when we were doing as much damage to ourselves as we were to a bottle of Black Jack. I was doing the same job then that I am now, but now I want a clue where the gold is."

"What do I have to do with this? My life isn't any of your business. You don't have anything of any interest in me other than to have spent a lot of time proving that our tax dollars have once

7

again been wisely spent. I'm done here for the night and there's a lovely lady who's been waiting for me to come home, and you surely have prior obligations because there must still be a lot of flies out there waiting to have their wings pulled off. You've had more than one clue already, and you've got the resources for finding out lots more of what isn't your business, so use them. And for your information, I don't particularly favor Black Jack. That and a Harley-Fergusson are the two most over-rated items on the American market. I'd put a BMW 750-R and a jug of Jim Beam against them any day of the week. I think you have me confused and it must be with somebody who cares. I never found gold around here, and neither has anybody else. Gold has been found everywhere around Estes Park other than in this valley, but gold has never been found in Estes Park. You'll have to leave now because I'm going to leave now and you don't need to be in the kitchen anymore. Good night."

"Aren't you even curious about how I learned what I know about you?"

"I find it depressing to wonder why anybody would want to waste their time finding out anything as mundane as what's going on with somebody else's life, but if I put it off as a bad Oprah day then perhaps it makes sense."

"There is a system open to Law Enforcement Agencies called NCIC, an abbreviation for "National Criminal Investigation Center", and it's a kick in the pants to play with because if you have the right access codes you can learn almost anything about anyone. Give it a name and Social Security Number and it'll tell you not only the last time that person pissed in an alley but the names of any winos passed-out in the cardboard boxes that got soggy. The Feds picked up most of the tab for setting it up because they had most of the information and it came under some dumb "Interstate" clause, but local cops pay their fair share for using it and the Feds get anything we get.

"Then you're not a Fed?"

"NYPD. Once I learned that I needed to keep my Ace Detectives on a leash and knew I was going to come here, I used it to look up an Italian restaurant in this area. Then I looked up a waiter at random from that restaurant, and since you are the only full-time male on the staff, your name won. Your background was so sketchy

8

that I got curious and looked further, and guess what I found? You are a rather complex person, and I don't think you want to go home yet"

"Look, I'm not so naive that I think what you're saying doesn't exist. In fact, if it didn't exist somebody should invent it. I mean, I could find some entertainment value in finding out who my waiter was going to be in the next town, but don't you have a job? Out of blind curiosity, did you look me up on your own time? Obviously, the bill for the time you spent on the company computer won't be billed to your home, but did you use the equipment on your own time? I'm just not into doing either crime or police work. I'm not going to crawl around under anything in order to satisfy you that what doesn't exist doesn't exist, and I sure won't do it on private property without permission. If I was willing to do any of that, I wouldn't tell a cop about it any more than I'd tell a cop that I was going to drink and drive, which I don't do either. You've got the wrong chump for the job."

"I never called you a chump. The only chumps I work with are the ones who wear badges and I don't have any choice about that. And you are the right one for the job."

"Right what, chump?"

"No, not chump, and let's drop that word. You're the right person for the job because you seem to be the only person for the job. What do you think I've been doing every time I've come out here for the last ten years, browsing the Teddy Bear Shops? I've found a reason to come here three times on business that could have been handled by somebody else and two of my vacations have been spent here. I can't find that quartz-bearing rock you talked about, and now I want you to find it for me."

"First, I haven't prospected, as you seem to know, in over ten years. I'm rusty to the point that I have forgotten almost everything I ever learned about it. Second, if you looked for it for so long in such a concentrated area and didn't find it, you ought to have convinced yourself by now that it doesn't exist. Most importantly, though, is what would you do with it once you found it? I mean, it's not like you could do a lot of hard-rock mining around the foundation of a hundred-thousand square-foot building without catching somebody's eye. Yeah, when I worked in the kitchen there

9

I was given carte-blanche to go anywhere on the grounds to look for minerals, and I did. It was fun to crawl around under the buildings, and I may have even found a thing or two they didn't know existed, like a walled-up room that isn't on the blueprints, but it was a dusty, dirty, dangerous way to spend my time and I didn't do much of it. Besides, the maintenance crew and I got along just fine and while they couldn't stop me I could tell they didn't think much of me crawling around their steam and water and gas lines. As for gold, I wouldn't have told the greedy bastards who owned the hotel about it if I did find any, and I sure as shit wouldn't have told anybody else."

"But you must have told somebody else or I wouldn't know about it. And I do know about it whether you want to admit that to me or not because you know about it and can't deny that it exists, at least not to yourself. We're not getting anywhere talking like this, though, and I have to put 'Tom Swift and his Electric Idiot' to bed. You going to work tomorrow night? Maybe we can get started off on a better foot once we both sleep on it."

What the hell. He knew about the rock and I couldn't keep on denying that it existed. I didn't have to tell him where it was, but my curiosity about how he found out about it was at a peak although I knew the story about Jack Daniels was manure. "Okay, but I expect to be busy enough that I doubt I could talk to anyone before nine thirty at the earliest. I'll sleep on it."

"Sounds good. I left the money and the check on the table, that okay?"

"Fine. I'll get it when I clear the table."

"Great, Jimmy. By the way, my name's Paul, but most people call me Pauli. See you tomorrow night," he said, holding out his hand.

Returning a handshake is an automatic reaction in this business because you never can tell what may be in the offered hand. This time it was empty, but that's not always the case. The guy was actually smiling as he herded the other two out the door. It was easy to see who was the drinker in that group because if he was a little lit, they were smashed. Maybe they'll smash the car into an Elk on the way back to their hotel. Welcome to the High Country.

*   *   *   *   *

People from New York City have earned a reputation for themselves as the pushiest, rudest, most obnoxious people this side of France, and they have cultured that well-deserved reputation to almost an art-form. That's a generalization, of course, but is a fair one which few New Yorkers I have ever met would deny, and I love them for it because when all is said and done, the one aspect of their pomposity which manifests itself around waiters is that they know how to tip. Unlike most waiters, I don't keep a running account of my tips throughout the evening because I find that can be very depressing. It also takes up my time and wouldn't change anything except for the worse because if I'm depressed while I'm on the floor my guests will sense it and the tips will drop even more. So I don't keep track of my tips, but occasionally one of them just reaches out and touches me and the one from the Cop on Table Four was one of those. I don't doubt that he was trying to impress me but being from New York puts a different perspective on what a favorable impression would be than from somebody from, say, Des Moines. I would definitely give him my ear tomorrow night, but how much he would get out of me would remain to be seen. The good cop-bad cop in this case might be the same guy, but I didn't see how it could matter. The main reasons for me being quiet about the gold for this long had gone away when the former owners of the hotel sold the place last month and left town and The Oliver Hotel, I'd heard, had fallen into such a state of disrepair that it might not be salvageable without a major rebuild. That would be a shame, to have those beautiful old buildings gone into such a state of ruin, but you don't dump your last dollar into a losing property just before you sell it. I'll have to take a look at it. Another time. What I have to do now is finish closing this puppy down and get home to that black-eyed ragamuffin who I hope I haven't kept waiting too long.. This has been one of those nights when I could find it easy to put my butt down and my feet up after work.

Chapter Two

Gold is yellow and pretty and everybody likes it, but it's a strange stuff, gold is. It brings out the best and the worst in a person, it makes and breaks friendships, kingdoms, and rules, but it never tarnishes itself. The oldest civilizations were adorned with it wrapped around priceless jewels and Science Fiction adorns outer-space Aliens in it wrapped around senseless fantasy. It was the lure of gold that settled the American West; it wasn't by coincidence that California became a State-of-the-Union sixty three years before its' next door neighbor Arizona. "Keep California Green and Golden" has been plastered on roadside signs in the Southwest since the turn of the Century. As many and varied economic philosophies as there are in all the Communist or Imperialist or Democratic nations on Earth, the one thing upon which they all agree is that gold is the place to be and they're so fearful of losing it that they all put it in a jail called Fort Knox where nobody even gets to look at it, much less play with or sculpture or even fondle it. King Tut to King George, what's the big deal? While only silver is a more efficient conductor of electricity, gold's so soft it can be squished to a transparent five-millionths of an inch thick which should have told the first person making something from it that it's basically without value. A huge hoax mankind has perpetrated on itself, but there's no accounting for taste so gold is still considered attractive in some social circles. The price it commands is ludicrously steep when you consider that other than in a few industrial applications it is pretty much useless, but it does command a ludicrously steep price and therefore the demand is always high. And that demand is why I found myself back on the Oliver Hotel property for the first time in almost ten years, snooping around while trying to look like any other tourist who might occasion to stroll around the grounds immersing themselves in a fantasy world of Contrived History. The history of the hotel is fascinating to say the least, but I wasn't imagining myself sipping tea on the veranda while hob-nobbing with Tom Edison and his pals. My fantasy world is certainly contrived, but the difference is that mine comes in two parts.

Sure, I was trying to put myself back to the beginning of the Century like everybody else who came here to dream, but my dreams settled on a different aspect of it. I was trying to recognize the mind-set of the people who had built this place, to see if I could distinguish any trends or nuances singular to the time. That's why I call it a fantasy, but it's an interesting exercise that might lead to some understanding which may be important later. The other part was trying to recreate the attitudes of the guys who dug the foundations to the buildings The original owner was said to be accepted with the local gentry, but he was following Lord Dunraven and even Richard Nixon could have beaten Dunraven at the popularity polls. Full of Pompous British Nobility, Dunraven had, thirty five years earlier, tried to make the entire valley his personal private hunting preserve and make the locals his personal private vassals. You couldn't do that in this area back then and make many local friends, so when Mr. Oliver built his hotel by hiring local labor from the town and paying a living wage he naturally moved to the top of the popularity heap as the town darling, at least publicly. But what had the workers said about him once they got home at night? It isn't uncommon for someone to work for one company all his life and never miss a day of belly-aching about it. What was the level of loyalty found in his employees; would it extend to revealing a vein of gold that they wouldn't get for themselves anyway? Did they just take home what they found and keep quiet about it or did they simply miss it altogether and never have any gold in their pockets to talk about? Superstition abounds in prospecting circles, especially among the lesser educated, and the guys who lived in these hills in 1905 working as part-time laborers were probably not the cream of the crop. They were doing back-breaking labor double-jacking rock and might have scorned the idea of hoisting that nine-pound hammer even one more time than necessary, regardless of the reason. That's considering that they recognized the gold for what it was, which they probably did not.

Mention gold prospecting to almost anyone and the first vision conjured in the mind is a grizzled, bearded old coot squatting in a creek scooping sand into a pan. That's certainly the most highly visible method of prospecting, but unless the gold happens to be near a creek it isn't a too efficient method of finding it. Gold is moved

13

across the surface of the Earth by the water and wind, but it is brought to the surface by hitchhiking in quartz. Quartz is a pretty hard rock, to which anybody who ever ate a sandwich at the beach will attest, but it is almost plasma so far as the crust of the Earth is concerned and gets slowly-but-surely squeezed to the surface at a fairly steady rate, carrying gold with it. When you see an inch-thick vein of quartz that is almost yellow, you get excited. When you're prospecting and see an inch-thick vein of quartz that is almost yellow, you get extremely excited and hope Mother Nature isn't playing one of her silly little games with you, for Mother's sense of humor is evidenced nowhere as it is with gold. First she tantalizes us with it, then she buries the little bit she has. She plays hide-and-seek with it, letting us catch a fleeting yellow glimpse now and then only to cloak it's location under a blanket of stone, and when she feels that our interest is beginning to wane she'll put a pot of it at the feet of some hapless blockhead who makes the rest of us realize how easily it could have been our pot of gold if only we had tried a little harder. That's what I'm doing here now, trying a little harder, trying to find the same chunk of rock that I had seen before and then trace back to it's likely origin through matching color and grain structure. It had struck me as so obviously gold-bearing when I first saw it that my first reaction was to look over my shoulder to see who else was running up behind me to grab it first. Where it was positioned in the top row of a two-foot high, fifty-foot long retaining wall would have made it obvious in it's absence if I had removed it, and so I decided to leave it where it was. After all, it had been sitting there for over three generations and nobody had messed with it yet, so I took the gamble that it would still be there when I got around to being serious with whatever it was that I would eventually decide to do about it. What I wasn't going to do about it was to tell the owners of the hotel. Those greedy bastards reeked of something unsavory, and it would be very simple to see those clowns removing the hotel or at least it's out-buildings in the name of "gold fever".

"Gold fever" is an expression often tossed around, but unless you have a lot of time on your hands you don't want to experience it. It becomes an all-encompassing passion that occupies not only your waking hours but creeps into your dreams and won't let go of your soul until you walk away from all prospecting and never look back.

That may sound a little poetic to anyone who has never experienced it, but anyone who has ever been grabbed by "gold fever" may think the description a bit subdued. It took me two months of working fourteen-hour days in the kitchen of the hotel to stop it from leading me around by my nose, and I don't know how much influence my aversion to the hotel owners had. I actually wasn't so worried about the buildings being dismantled because the Hotel is registered as an "Historical Place" by the Feds and it couldn't be taken down, but there isn't a ninety year old, four story, wood frame building in the world that doesn't have the capacity to burn to the ground, and do it fast.

The Oliver Hotel doesn't encourage anyone other than registered guests to wander around the grounds. Maybe they think that such a policy will encourage more people to stay with them, but for whatever reason it has always been their policy and they are so adamant about it that a few years ago they charged a $5.00 fee just to drive onto the property. That one backfired on them unmercifully, but they still invite "outsiders" to the Hotel only to attend such social functions as Piano or String Recitals, the tickets to which, by the way, usually run about $5.00 each. What that boiled down to was that a major obstacle I was going to need to overcome before I could do anything was to be able to get on the grounds at all. I could walk in from town, but this time of year when the Hotel is enjoying about five percent occupancy the paranoid Front Desk Spooks know every correct face, and I would immediately be spotted as "residentially incorrect". The best way I could come up with to approach the problem would be the old "hide in plain sight" ploy, and hope I got away with it.

Almost everybody likes old cars, and old hotels seem to have a special affection for them; that was going to be my key. For the last four years I have been restoring a 1948 Plymouth for no reason other than a restoration is something I have always wanted to do. I didn't have any particular affinity toward Plymouths when I started the project, and Walter P. Chrysler has probably spun in his grave more than once for some of the language I've used since the first time I laid a wrench on it and scraped half the skin off my knuckles, but the drive-train is now as close to perfect as it's going to get and if you squint at the body from half a mile away in poor light it could pass for almost finished, so I cruised up their driveway and parked in the lot marked "Visitors". This lot isn't paved and it's several hundred yards from the front door, but it is still in the line of sight of the Hotel Lobby so I could rest assured that my arrival wouldn't go unnoticed. As I said, when I began restoring "PIGIRON" (a nickname the two-and-a-half-ton beast earned for itself) I was doing it as a lark, but as the project progressed so did my enthusiasm and I started becoming "Mr. Plymouth-Head". I put a "Mopar Parts" thermometer outside my front door, hung a "Mopar Parts" sign on the door to my shop, and accessorized myself with a navy-blue double-breasted pin-stripe suit, gray felt Fedora, and wing-tip shoes. That was the regalia in which I had adorned myself as I opened the front door of the Oliver Hotel, strutted my stylin' stuff across the foyer, and sidled into the bar. It didn't surprise me that the joint was empty in the middle of the afternoon because it isn't exactly what you'd call a "destination bar", but I figured that somebody would show up eventually. Who I didn't expect it to be was somebody I knew, or worse, somebody who knew me.

"Jimmy, that has got to be the silliest looking sack of rags I've ever seen you wear, but it goes with the car. Nice to see you, buddy. What you doing up here, trying to keep a low profile? What can I get you?"

Classic bartender. Two statements, one question, and then take an order.

"A Bud to start. As always, Judy, other than being cursed with an abnormally small penis, things aren't too bad. When did you start here?"

One thing about waiting tables in a small tourist town is that you will eventually work with most of the other locals who do the same thing because of the transient nature of the job; everybody thinks he can run a restaurant so there are always a lot of new ones opening where the old ones closed and the demand for waitstaff during the height of the season is so great that few questions are asked and rumors are ignored. Judy was one of those people who had a true gift for dealing with the public but wasn't dedicated enough to last very long at one place. She was a warm body who would pull six shifts a week and could be expected to make all of them for her first two or three weeks and most of the rest thereafter,

16

so she could usually be found working somewhere in town. You could just never know where to expect to see her. Today I saw her behind the bar at the Oliver Hotel.

"You know how it is. I wouldn't sleep with Chef Seaton out at Pesto's so he started bad-mouthing me to Dino, and when I wouldn't sleep with him either they said I had my hand in the till. At least the new owners here are smart enough to ask my friends and learn the truth. You still out at the Da Vinci?"

I said it was a transient-waiter town, and that can't be driven home more realistically than listening to the typical greeting between members of that trade which asks if you are still working at the place you were working last week. "Yeah, I'm still out there, and when I leave it will be kicking and screaming."

"How are the new owners doing? Do they blow as hard as I hear they do?" Interesting choice of paraphrasing, coming from her. Judy has quite the reputation in some areas.

"Those are just the usual rumors, Judy. Sure there have been some changes, but there needed to be some changes, and I doubt that any of them will be noticeable to the people who eat there. How long have you been back here?

"How often you been back here to check? Just joking. I started about two weeks ago, just after the new owners took over. It's a job and my boss is gay so I don't have to worry about him. I like your car. You always dress like that when you drive it?"

"My understated alter-ego needs to break out now and then, regardless of how hard I try to keep it in check. No, actually that's the only car I have now. I like to keep a low profile so I thought I'd dude-it-up to come out here. Who has his hand on the button here now?" After you work in a town like this for a while there aren't too many questions you can't ask.

"Some geek from Florida named Robin that the new owners brought in. You want to meet him?"

"Not particularly, but I'd like to kind of feel comfortable walking around these beautiful old buildings without everybody watching me like an outsider".

"You are an outsider, Honey, and you always have been. Don't worry about anybody. We all saw you pull up and I told them you used to work here, so nobody's going to be watching you. The

17

catacombs are locked and so are the barracks, so figure that everything else is fair game."

"Thanks, kiddo. What does this place get for a bottle of Bud these days?"

"Nothing for the first one today. The boss likes your car, too."

"Cool", I said as I eased off the stool and slid a dollar next to the almost-empty bottle. Funny about tips; you can use a percentage as a base for the tip, but what you are really doing is paying a waiter for his time, and if you monopolize a waiter's time while you're having a $5.00 sandwich and then leave $1.00 thinking it's twenty percent, you've just ripped-off the waiter because he couldn't make any money with any other tables. On the other hand, any waiter who allows you to take up that much of his time is in dire need of retraining. I always tip well, and the service I get reflects it. "See you later. I'm going to browse around before it gets cold."

"Have fun. I'm out of here in fifteen minutes, so maybe I'll catch you down at the Wheel."

"Sounds good. See you there." The Wheel wasn't the original bar in town, but it had been around since Pontius was a Pilot and is the only place in town that prefers to be called a "saloon" rather than a "bar", which means that you can be about as stupid in there as you want, short of drugs and fighting. It also is the cheapest place in town to drink. Probably give it a miss today, though, because I have stuff to do and I like the place too much.

Yeah, I have stuff to do, and the occasion demands that I do it in broad daylight so that I could see what's going on. I'm searching for a foot-square chunk of rock that had been cut out of the ground in order to make room for the concrete foundation of one of the out-buildings of the hotel; the chunk of rock with an inch-thick vein of quartz that's almost yellow. Prospecting is a mixture of an exact science and blind luck, and there are rules for finding gold, but the raw truth is that 95% of the world's new gold is found as a secondary by-product of other mining, like for copper. Down in Southeastern Arizona, where I had done my earlier prospecting, employees of Phelps-Dodge and Anaconda float their findings to the little Chinese guy who shows up at one of the local hotels near Safford every third Thursday with triple beam balance scales set out on the bar in the lounge which might make somebody from anywhere other than a mining area think he was doing an overt drug trade. The trade he's doing may be almost as illegal, but no President ever spent billions to bust it and the local cops show up often enough with their own stuff that they don't see much of a crime in what is going on. That's what I'm counting on, this lack of seeing a crime, because ten years ago I found what I think is the first gold strike to ever hit this valley. It just happened to lie under a fine old historic landmark which denied me the access I would have needed to get it out and now I'm busy having a life and don't want to boogie around private property in order to share it with somebody else, not even Pauli the Pig.

*   *   *   *   *

The Retaining Wall reminded me of an episode one day last week, down at The Wheel. I was sitting at the bar reading a book, a habit I picked up in college when I lived in an unheated house and did my homework during winter in a warm bar with a pitcher of beer. I find most bar conversation to be lacking, but I like the atmosphere so I take a book with me and read until I run into somebody I really do want to talk with or until I'm ready to leave. A book also makes a great excuse to not talk to somebody I really don't want to talk with. So I was alternately reading and "mind-surfing" over the other people when I was struck by a head of the most beautiful auburn hair I think I have ever seen. It wasn't the extreme length that impressed me because almost anybody can do that, but it was perfect in every way. There was no visible parting in her hair; it just 'became' the cascade flowing evenly down the back and sides of her head, which was the part I could see. It followed the contour of her head, moving only enough to allow the trace of one milky-white ear to peek out at me, then tucked back to her neck. At her shoulder one mutinous lock went forward to flow over what I could only imagine while the remainder of that lustrous thatch curved between the blades of her shoulders to come to rest contentedly poised on the barstool behind her beautiful bottom. A person can become lost in elegance, but it's not polite to stare so I made it almost a full paragraph further into my book before I chanced

19

another glance, and by now she had finished her conversation and had turned to taste her wine. With her head tilted slightly back and her eyes nearly closed her profile could have been painted with three thin strokes of the artist's brush; one for her eyebrow, one for her lashes, and one for the lips sipping the wine. I didn't get much farther because I was absolutely captivated in what I was seeing and wanted only to drink in the hair and the lips and the eyebrow and the lights glistening from her eye. Lights glistening? Rats! She had seen me staring at her and was now looking right back at me. What I felt like doing was sticking my head up my butt and disappearing, but I think I was already doing that so I just meekly smiled. She smiled too, faintly at first but as my embarrassment became more obvious her smile widened, revealing teeth polished white. Revealing, too, the empty socket off to the side where one of those teeth should have been. The same way that retaining wall looked just now. A beautiful smile of cut stones following the contour of the hillside, but with one tooth missing. No wonder Pauli the Pig hadn't found it; it wasn't here, but judging by the erosion of the dirt it was supposed to buttress it hadn't been gone for too long. Rats again! From the look of the rest of the remaining wall, the rocks had been collected from more than one spot around here and I had been counting on the missing rock to give a clue as to where had been its' original home. If I didn't have to work tonight I might just head down to The Wheel just to see if Judy might have heard anything about it, but that's pretty far fetched anyway. Home, James, for lunch and employment await thee.

*   *   *   *   *

"So the rock is gone. You know there has to be more of the same around there somewhere, so let's go find it."

"There's one fundamental problem you have not yet addressed, Pauli, and I doubt you're even aware that the problem exists. That rock was the key to this whole thing, and without another one just like it we had just as well satisfy ourselves that it would have been a fun treasure hunt and let it go at that." Sunday night has always been my favorite night of the week to wait tables. The screaming kids are for the most part back home or at least on

20

their way to it, and the people who do come out are relaxed and want only to enjoy a quite, calm meal. It isn't generally so lucrative as Friday or Saturday, but the pace isn't nearly as hectic and I get to spend more time with my guests which translates into a higher tip percentage. I don't count my tips during my shift, but tips are what I do for a living. On top of that, the owner gives us an open bar after work on Sunday. We usually don't abuse it, but this Sunday may prove to be different. Pauli had come back and was obviously in a better frame of mind. I'm sure a lot of that had to do with having already sent his subordinates down to Ft. Collins to await the release of their prisoner in the morning, but I think he was expecting good news from me, too.

"It isn't as though I could waddle down to the BLM Office and stake a claim. We'd need to satisfy the "Prudent Man" clause, and without an assay from that rock it just couldn't be done."

"I'm a prudent man. I've been a cop for over twentyfive years, and a prudent one, too."

"You don't get it. The "Prudent Man" clause states that you need to prove that a "prudent man" could make a "prudent living" by mining the claim." True to government form, the word "Prudent" is never defined anywhere other than in the mind of the person authorized to demand that you prove it. It can be done anytime from the time you file your claims to until you patent the land, but the choice of when it needs to be done is decided by the Powers-That-Be, not by the prospector. "We wouldn't be able to patent the land anyway, just claim the mineral rights, so you can bet that it would have to be proved right away. Like, we could save everybody a lot of trouble if we could just take the assay with us when we filed the claim."

"You mean that we have to tell them there's gold there and wait for them to decide if we can claim it?"

"They can't do it quite that fast. They'd let us file the claims, then ask us to prove them. Shouldn't take them more than just a few hours to chase us back up the hill. Look, I had some friends who were ski bums who came up with the brilliant scheme that if they filed some mining claims they could build their own personal ski resort and not need to pay for the land. One of them even remembered to file near a creek. They had barely gotten the foundation of the building laid out in their minds when up walks a Ranger with a gold pan in his hand, wanting to know where all the gold was. The guy closest to him couldn't talk because he still had part of the joint he had tried to swallow when he first saw the Ranger in his mouth, so he just pointed at a spot at random on the creek bank and shrugged. After all, he was a skier, not a miner. The kindly Ranger scooped some sand into his pan and within a few minutes found three nuggets the size of his fingernail. From that point on my friends never had to work another day in their lives, but that isn't going to happen to us. The rock is gone and we don't have any nuggets to pan out of a creek. We don't even have a creek, unless you count the one we'd be up if we pursue this venture. Why don't we lift a toast to what could have been and let it go at that?"

"I don't want to let it go at that! I've put too much into this!"

"So has every clown who ever tried to find The Lost Dutchman Mine or any other fairy tale which deals with 'I deserve to be rewarded for my efforts'. The Great American Excuse for not realizing The Great American Dream. Bust your butt and pay your taxes and go to church and Honor Thy Father and Mother, you know, the stuff they teach you in school when they weren't teaching you to fear annihilation of the World at the touch of a Big Red Button in the middle of the night. What do they teach now that the Ruskies bit the dust?"

"They teach you that cops are your friends, which makes about as much sense. Jimmy, cops aren't your friends and they aren't trying to be. They're the guys you call to get into a fight for you, then you get to spit on them whether they win or lose. I don't want to be a cop anymore. I want to hit the Mother Lode and find a sweet little nineteen-year-old who loves me for my money and makes no bones about it. I think I don't want to give up on this property just yet."

"Then don't give up. Keep beating a dead horse long enough and you'll grow Popeye arms. As for me, I kinda like the idea of pursuing this thing but I need some gold up front. Gold that has come from the property in at least a semi-legal manner. However you get it, you must remember that the BLM isn't the Veteran's Administration; these guys are serious professionals and will expect you to conduct yourself in the same manner. Treat them with respect and don't try to get clever with them or they'll have your gonads on a pole in the town square."

"I'm a cop, remember? Don't need to lecture me on it. It just irritates me greatly. Who do you think got the rock?"

"I don't know. They go through dozens of transient workers from all over the world in the summer. Everybody here does. Maybe one of them took it as far as it was convenient and left it in an airport on the way back to Heathrow. Who do you think took it?"

"A local. Somebody who knew what he was looking for and where to find it, and didn't want to share it with anybody else. Somebody who wanted to wait until I left to score for himself. Somebody greedy."

"Pauli," I said, standing and no longer in the mood to drink with this guy, "you carry a gun and even without it I don't think I could get drunk enough to figure I could whip you in a fight, and with that in mind, blow me! I didn't take your stupid rock, and I don't want to be a part of your stupid dream!"

Chapter Three

There is nothing wrong with greed. Not really. We're all taught to abhor it's vile name from an early age and given moral lessons of the inherent evil of greed, but greed can be your friend. To say that greed is bad is a lot like saying that money is bad; a lack of greed is a way of keeping those who don't have any money satisfied that they are better persons for being broke. The hole in that argument is that, next to food and shelter, greed is the strongest motivator humans possess, and to stifle it is an unnatural reaction. Rejoice in greed. Embrace greed. Face the music. Join the club.

Pauli the Pig had become one with greed; he was as greedy for that gold as he had eggs to hatch and cats to kill. It was the driving force behind his life, his motivation to get out of bed for something other than to take his morning dump, and he was loving every minute of it. Pauli had tasted greed, and in doing so had brushed against The Black Side of Greed; that side which motivates a person to do what he would never normally do. Like The Black Side of Hunger which would compel a hungry man to steal food from a starving child. What would you do if you were hungry enough, kill for it? Endangered species would go out the window, that's a given, and a Spotted Owl might be yummy for the tummy. Would you kill another person for it? Sure. Eat a whole South American Rugby Side (they were Rugby players, not Soccer players) and let The World say you're justified. What would you do if you're greedy enough? Could killing be justified for greed? The Black Side of Greed? Who would try to justify that? Somebody had pulled that trigger.

Greed had gotten Pauli the Pig out of New York City more times than anything else in his life, an action that in-and-of-itself should be worth any price. It made him use his mind, and the exercise he got from scrambling around the hills probably added years to his life. Greed was good for him. Greed was making him a pain in my butt, but that was my problem, not his. The man had more spirit than he was supposed to have, and you can't fault greed for that. If there's any fault to be assigned, it has to go to his inability to visualize the reality of his quest, but no quest for gold has ever had much of a foothold in reality so there can't be much fault to assign. I hate to be too discouraging to him because of all the good he seems to be getting out of it, but the point at which I'm going to bow-out is rapidly approaching. I told him about that stupid rock against my better judgment. I agreed to look for that stupid rock against my better wishes. I've already gotten myself more involved than I have ever had any interest to do, and now he's implied very strongly that I'm a thief. That pretty much frosts it, far as I'm concerned. I spent three and a half years on a treasure hunt of my own, and if I wanted to do it again I wouldn't invite an up-tight, frustrated, gun-carrying New York City Cop to go with me. I probably wouldn't invite anybody to go with me, and greed has nothing to do with why not.

I used to think that the biggest headache involved with prospecting was the physical act of prospecting itself, but I was wrong. The biggest headache involved in prospecting is the hangers-on; those clowns who lash themselves to you and want to come along for the ride but are never willing to do their share of what it takes to actually prospect. I've run more than one of them out of my camp, and I don't feel like strapping-on another. Gathering firewood takes a minimal amount of time when you're in virgin territory, but it does take time away from anything else. I have the act of cooking campfire meals down to such a fine science that it would make a college student blush, but it does take time away from everything else. Do it yourself, Pauli, and open your eyes to the real world of prospecting. I don't want to start all over again, and I certainly don't want to teach some tyro how to re-invent the wheel. I've had more than one lady approach me and say something to the effect of, "Jimmy, you know all about living in the mountains. Would you teach me to go camping?" Sounds like an inviting situation, but have you ever been in the company of a person who was normal in every way other than, lacking a porcelain throne and flower-scented toilet paper, refuses to evacuate her bowels? The third day of that situation is not a pretty sight to see, and since the first time that happened it has been a requirement for anybody who wants to go into the hills with me, male or female, to squat behind a rock or a tree and just shit. I won't have watch them do it, but if they can't go then they can't go. Not with me, and it's not negotiable. I'm done with it, and I hope that Pauli will find something in his life to make him feel as good about himself as prospecting does so long as it isn't looking for that one particular vein. To continue that pursuit would do nothing other than to chase himself into an early grave.

*　　*　　*　　*　　*

Consider for a moment why any city gets started originally. Seacoast towns were the first to be settled because that's where the settlers landed, but the specific sites speak of good harbors where rivers met the sea. Inland cities needed a different draw. Rivers were still the strong suit, but where there weren't rivers there still needed to be water, and where there was water there needed to be some form of commerce to support the folks huddled around the town fountain. Denver began as a trading post for the fur trappers who wanted to swap pelts for a round-trip ticket back to the hills. The South Platte River isn't really what anyone would call navigable, but a few feet from the North bank was a straight shot 860 miles downhill to St. Louis and the Mississippi River, and the railroads filled that gap by the Civil War. Easy access, and that's why Denver.

Why Estes Park? There was never any mining here, and the Beaver population could have been taken to it's practical limit within a few years. Why Estes Park at all? Here's why: Hunting and fishing and the notoriety that goes with rubbing elbows with the rich-and-famous. Good press. Blind luck. That's why Estes Park, and it has been running on one string of blind luck after another for so many years that the Town Fathers now think they deserve it, as their actions have repeatedly shown. Maybe like a movie star who is so popular that he thinks he's worth several million bucks for a cameo spot in a movie, or a real estate agent who thinks he's worth seven percent of an inflated sale. Nonsense and rubbish to be sure, but the prevalent thought. The root of the problem. The root of the problem that allowed Low Stakes Gambling to pass the local vote because tricky-wording made the people trying to shoot-it-down pass it with an outstanding majority. The root of the problem that found

John Loughlin dead in front of his Bank, laying by the open doors one morning after a .25-06 slug had passed easily through his heart and spent the dying moments of it's trajectory doing cartwheels inside his rib cage. The root of the problem, and it was our problem gone berserk.

Every "Dirty Old Man" wants two things; he wants every attractive High School girl to be a virgin and he wants her to want him to change that status. That's why Dirty Old Men's clubs sponsor parades that exhibit this year's crop of virgins down Main Street in skimpy clothing during cold weather. It has nothing to do with a tightly erect nipple compressed into a well-rounded-but-not-fully-developed breast. Now there was one less Dirty Old Man.

The ambulance had taken Loughlin's body to the hospital by the time the Bank was open for 'business as usual'. Mr. Loughlin had held the only set of keys to the building, and in his position of President and Chief Executive Officer of the Bank, Vice President-Loans, President of Rotarians, Member of the Town Council, Founding Member of the Historical Society, and Lifetime Member of The VFW (he rarely attended), John Loughlin's true function in life was to open the doors to the Bank. He will be sorely missed in this capacity, but for the rest of the town there were deposits to be made and checks to cash and homes to buy. The cops and the curious were still there en mass but had huddled into little separate groups to talk nervously amongst themselves. Maybe the crowd thinks it would be disrespectful to their fallen comrade to leave but the wind-chill factor has it's own little way of changing one's perspective on what is and what isn't disrespectful. I expect the place will clear out before too long. Eventually one of the bystanders might have the brainstorm to look around the cliff 200 yards to the south for a spent cartridge, but that was to be in the future if at all. For now the mood in-and-outside the Bank was somber, a time of quiet reflection, a period of stillness, a moment of suppressed giggles. John Loughlin was not well liked around these parts regardless of his social stature, and while most would agree that it was too bad a murder had happened in our sleepy little town, most would also not attend his Memorial Service.

*   *   *   *   *

Little towns can have an incredibly complex social hierarchy, much more so than large towns, or at least much more visible. In the case of Estes Park, there are four distinct social classes, four "fiefdoms", which have rules of their own and allegiances within themselves, and each thinks that he is the top of the heap. Estes is a one-industry town, and that industry always has been and probably always will be Tourism. From Estes's inception it has been the tourists who have brought the new money to town, and come September when the tourists left, almost every source of income left with them. To this end, very few people living here in Summer stayed in town during the Winter, and those who did usually had a rough time of it. Even the wealthier ones lived in the silent terror that for some reason the tourists wouldn't come back in the Spring in time to replenish the coffers. Businesses catering to tourists shut their doors behind the last tourist leaving town, and their owners followed the tourists down the hill. Year-around businesses like the grocery store or the Bank had to be willing to extend a lot of credit during the thin months, but that's how they all stayed afloat. As late as 1932, when Main Street was paved for the first time, the number of families living here all year numbered only about three dozen and few of their homes were heated by much more than a fireplace. Some of the children in those families still live in Estes Park because during the Great Depression those families found a way to stay. They'd take money from the tourists during the Summer and trade that money between themselves during the Winter, and they stayed. They organized themselves and their town in such a way that they could stay, and by the end of The Second World War when there was some money back into the national economy and gasoline was no longer rationed and the tourists began using both money and gas to visit Estes Park, who do you think was there to feed them and put them up for the night? Right. The few families who had found a way to stick around the town and invest in the land and the buildings and their future became the "First Fiefdom" of Estes, the "Ruling Class", and if they began to developed a bit of cynicism during the ensuing decades when a lot of new people started showing up and taking pre-made jobs and calling the town "theirs", who's to blame them? People showing up and bitching about the Phone Company

28

not supplying enough lines, people bringing in crime and drugs, people bringing in other people. The little town needed more people in order to grow, but until the newcomers learned to treat the town with the respect it deserves they'll get little respect for themselves.

They don't call themselves "The First Fiefdom", nor do they consider themselves to be "The Ruling Class", and they're not any more rude or snobbish than a cross section of any group of people. They were and are the original people who paved the way for everyone else and if they are considered by anyone to be a Fiefdom, it is only because of and in comparison to the three other Fiefdoms which have grown around them.

*   *   *   *   *

"I'm not surprised", offered Jody into his morning Budweiser. That was the general mood in The Wheel, reminiscent of when Hinkley shot President Reagan; people were shocked that it had happened and dismayed at another assassination attempt, but nobody was surprised. That it was John Loughlin was irrelevant because there weren't too many of the "Old-Guard Powers That Be" who were well liked in town anymore. They had all been a little too tricky the last few years, shown too much of The Black Side of Greed, and by now the townsfolk had their fill of being taxed with nothing to show for it except over-crowded schools staffed with underpaid teachers and a Police Force twice the size it needed to be and a gambling law that nobody wanted. The situation of the teachers was dismissed easily with the notion that they didn't need much pay because they had the beauty of the area to compensate them. I think not. Ever try to eat a Pine Tree or pay the rent with a Mountain? Whenever the question of the cops came up we were reminded of the millions of Summer tourists who need their assistance, but that argument loses something in it's translation when you consider the dozen or so college students brought in every summer to keep "the cattle" from wandering off the sidewalks and into the streets. The City Fathers have been blatantly lying to us for too long, and every year the dose we're expected to swallow becomes increasingly large and increasingly bitter. John Loughlin found out this morning just how bitter it is.

"Jimmy, what do you think ?"

"Huh?" Snappy response, but I was elsewhere.

"What do you think about this morning?"

"I think the entire Town Council should be removed from office by impeachment and dragged naked and screaming down Main Street. I wouldn't imagine many of them would be immune from criminal charges, but perhaps assassination is a bit extreme. Not everyone, so it seems, would agree with me on that last point. I think that anybody given enough rope will fuck things up, and I think somebody just fucked things up."

"Shooting Loughlin was no mistake. The only thing that S. O. B. did in this town was line his pockets."

"If everyone who'd been called an 'S. O. B.' in this town got shot, it'd make a terrible stench. Maybe now the State will begin to answer some of those letters they've been getting with more than a reminder to vote. It'll be interesting to attend the next Council meeting. Which one do you think's pissing-himself right about now?"

"They all should be." Jody had been in 'Nam about the same time I had and I knew he came away a non-violent person. Speaking like that wasn't like him. "I wouldn't do it and I don't know anybody who would, but I could list a couple dozen people who'll buy the bullets." Like most folks who pounded nails or slung food in this town, Jody had a college degree. His, Political Science, should have given him better insight than condoning murder, especially a political murder, but that looks like the direction he's going. "Those clowns must think we're pretty dumb for us to have not caught on to what they were doing."

"All of us know what's been going on, Jody, or haven't you seen the 'Letters To The Editor' pages in the last two months?" Marlin the bartender was in strange form, like he actually was interested in what response each person gave to each question. And there had been lots of questions. How he can maintain that demeanor while talking to a bunch of beer-swilling noon-time drinkers is beyond me, but I'm not the one who's doing it. Now he was waxing philosophic. "There's a Japanese axiom which states that once you must resort to violence, you have already lost the battle. Strange breed of people to come up with something like that,

30

the Japanese, considering their actions in this century alone, but it sounds good to me. That philosophy should apply to anywhere, but I guess it don't."

"Yeah, I guess it don't, Marlin. Not here in Estes, anyway. You get the feeling something's going to happen?"

"No. Something has already happened and I thought maybe you were in on it."

"Not me", I said. "Not yet. I don't want to get too weird and then trust an unknown to have my name on his list". I don't really want to get too weird at all, and shooting John Loughlin is just too weird. For Pete's sake, I live here to not have to lock my door or watch my back. Everybody has a cause. The Blacks blame Whitey, Whitey blames the Mexicans, everybody blames the Feds, and nobody likes the Jews. Same story been going around for years and it doesn't make any more sense now than a hundred years ago or a hundred years in the future. You got troubles? Blame them on anyone other than yourself. Find a scapegoat, a sacrificial lamb. It's sick and wrong. What a narrow, tiny little world this is.

*   *   *   *   *

"Where we going?" For a guy who's spent a quarter-century of being what he referred to as "a prudent cop", Pauli has done it in style. His model of Jaguar ran close to five figures last year. I have a friend who bought one, and he let me drive it once. Nothing more spectacular than piloting the Space Shuttle until you do this wiggling thing with the "go" pedal, and then all Hell breaks loose. Nice drive. A man needs to be slammed-back into his seat at Mach .79 now and then in order to appreciate the finer things in life. Speed is one of those finer things. It puts everything into perspective when the only thing you have to lose is your life, and at many miles-per-hour on a mountain road you can rapidly come to the realization that your life is all you've really got. A calming effect, speed. Rest in peace or rest in pieces. I love it, but I wouldn't want to do it for a living. I like to watch Fitipaldi and some of the Andrettis and a whole bunch of the Unsers, but I mostly want to watch. Voyeuristic racing works for me, but Pauli the Pig has the wheel and Jimmy the Geek has the thrill. Yahoo! Where did that come from?

31

"You got a problem in this town, Jimmy, and somebody had better do something pretty quick or it's all going down the tubes. Two thumbs down. Get involved for your own sake. This is the time to do it."

"The way I look at it, the Old Guard are all going to be in retirement before long. Their kids will take over a lot of their ideals, but they'll have some thoughts of their own, some fresh concepts, a Second Feifdom, if you will. Other folks are going to sell-out to beat taxes. It's a fluid situation, and I don't own any more of it than anyone else who doesn't like it. It's going to run it's course and we at the bottom of the heap are going to gripe and still depend on getting a paycheck at the end of the week, and that paycheck is what counts. Killing anybody isn't going to add to that."

"To be so young and naive must be a joy. This whole valley is on the edge of a violent revolution, and you don't even recognize it. I'm glad I got a job."

Grab second gear at 70 MPH and vent frustrations on the road. How many of us want to do that right now? Go for it, Bambi, step out into the headlights and get blinded right about (4... 3... 2... 1...) *NOW!*

*　　*　　*　　*　　*

The town of Nederland is a mining town and has been since it's inception. It wouldn't mind getting some of the overflow from the other places in the Front Range of the Rockies where so many tourists jamb the towns and let go of those touro-dollars, but the two or three gift shops in the town have actual gifts rather than rubber tomahawks, and the residents of Nederland are able to make a living and still have their town pretty much to themselves. They also have The Pioneer Inn, physically unlike The Wheel but the same attitude plus a great menu, and that's where we were headed for lunch. You don't look for a parking lot in Nederland. They've got a big one in the shopping center and several others scattered where they're needed, but this is still a small town. Almost pristine, if a town can be pristine. I'm not in love with the town, but it's a welcome change to the bump-and-grind hustle of Estes, a reminder of what Colorado

32

was before too many children gave birth to too many children. Where we parked was about twenty feet from the front door of The Pioneer which was neat because you don't drive through a small town, any small town, in a Black-on-Black-on-Black Jaguar Coupe and do so inconspicuously. I'll take a cheap thrill over no thrill any day, be it driving the car, being driven in the car, arriving in the car, or the women who might kiss me for a good ride in the car. That's a male view, of course, but I'm a male and it's the view I have. In my next incarnation I may look for something different. Right now I'm looking for lunch.

"What do you think is the biggest problem in the world today, Jimmy?" I had become more or less relaxed with Pauli. I had found out the easy way that he wasn't quite so prone to losing his temper as I had first thought, and when he did lose it he wasn't violent. At least toward me, and that's what counts. He'd asked me some off-the-wall questions on the drive out here, and I found them to be an enjoyable diversion to simply driving, if what we were doing could be called simply driving.

"In the whole world? Over-population, without a doubt. It's biblical in origin, but I don't quote scriptures. Over-population."

"I ain't heard anyone say that for years. Where'd you come up with that?"

"I subscribed to the notion that we already have enough people on this planet when I first heard about it around the time Neil Armstrong became famous, yet now that the Earth's population has again doubled it is no longer seen by the World as a problem. I believe that not only is population still a problem, but it is the most touchy, opinionated, misinformed problem ever to be posed to mankind; if it were not such a disturbing question we would not find it so disdainful a topic of conversation".

"Why don't you just back off a bit and relax?"

"Relaxing isn't the problem, and it isn't the answer either. And this problem won't get answered by offing bankers one at a time. I don't think this problem will ever get solved because humans are, in general, a very selfish breed who can't see past their own generation."

"You spend much time dwelling on over-population?"

"Almost none. It isn't up to me to solve it. I have zero children, and there's nothing more I can do about it, so I think about other things. The stuff that conceivably could be in my control."

"Like what?

"Like who's going to pay for lunch. Like how angry do you need to be at somebody before you kill them? John Loughlin wasn't a physical threat to anybody". Small in stature and obnoxious beyond belief, arrogant as Hell, and generally offensive to everybody, he was almost xenophobic and terminally shy, but not a threat. He could wield some power through the Loan Department, I guess, but he was above all a banker and would do whatever it took to earn money for his bank, and you don't earn much money for a bank by offending too many would-be borrowers. "Why do you think he got shot?"

"I've been a cop too many years to think you need a reason to get shot. People just *do* things, and as soon as we need an explanation for them we're not going to be a free country anymore. Look, this country is ruled by Anarchy. Nobody's going to admit it, but that's the way it is and it needs to stay that way if we're going to function as a Democracy."

"Pauli, you on drugs?"

"That question's a quick way to annoy a cop, but no. Think about it; in order for this country to be free, that means we turn loose a quarter of a billion people to come and go as they please. The law sets up guidlines, but those guidelines aren't enforced unless somebody strays too far out of them. That's what I do for a living, but there aren't any watchdogs herding the general public inside those lines, inside an imaginary fence. Nothing gets done until you step outside that fence, and then what does get done is pitifully little. Every person is on his own until then, in a state of Anarchy."

"Profound. Simplistic, but profound. Too bad nobody would buy it."

"Buy it? If the word ever got out about it there are some people in high places who would become very nervous. It isn't much of a secret, but it's sure not taught in school. The Big Boys who have thought of it, and believe me there aren't many of them, are counting on other distractions to keep our feeble minds occupied. Like creating Earth Day when Tricky Dick wanted to take attention away from the Viet Nam war. Or the 'Cold War', which had a lot more use than simply to justify nuclear proliferation. Russia may have had the capacity to nuke us to Photons, but they weren't as crazy as The Good Guys painted them to be. Now that they're gone, you notice a sudden frenzied interest in Domestic Economy? Ten years ago everybody had an opinion about the economy, and it was usually critical, but that's as far as it went. Economics is too deep and too dry to hold much interest for anyone very long, yet nowadays lots of otherwise normal people are losing too much sleep over it. Think that's an accident? The public *must* be fed bad news to keep their minds as busy as their minds are going to be or they might start using their minds for something that counts."

"Think that has anything to do with John Loughlin?"

"With any luck, John Loughlin's death was a random act", Pauli stated into the bite of his sandwich. "What your cops should be doing right now is spending at least as much time trying to find out the 'why' as much as the 'who'. That way, if it wasn't random, they could start taking steps to save some lives. They won't, though, because being a cop is like any other job. You got good ones and you got bad ones, but the vast majority have long since lost any idealism they brought into the Force when they joined, and are more than content to issue enough DUI's to make them look productive and leave the heavy thinking to someone else."

"That wouldn't be the voice of cynicism I hear, would it?"

"You bet," he munched, "and it's justified cynicism. You've got it too, only your hang-up is over-population. That doesn't mean either one of us are right or wrong, it just means that we see things in a different light that most people. I like being a cop, and I'm generally proud of what I've done and how I've done it, but for some reason I never got into that 'rut' that lulls most cops and everyone else to sleep by the time they hit their mid-thirties."

"Just out of curiosity, if you're so proud of what you've done, how do you explain driving a car that must have cost you three-years pay?"

"Easy. I don't. Family money bought it. I got an inheritance from a dead relative and I bought myself a toy. Don't think I wasn't asked to drop my pants and bend over for a thorough exam by the Department when I got it, either. It was a one-shot deal and I've had fun with it, but the insurance alone costs me nearly a new car every year. Let's go drive it, 'cause I've got to get back home by the end of the week and I want to be on the road by dark. I still have to deal with those silly-assed subordinates of mine in Ft. Collins today, too."

Pauli had not only left me with his business card when he went "down the hill" to meet his fellow New Yorkers, but he also dropped a couple of inadvertent tips. It's obvious that he likes the area, but I don't think Pauli thinks much of the town in general.

Chapter Four

There's a fine line separating "silly" from "silly-assed", and what I just saw was "silly-assed". Drinking is silly. Drinking and driving is silly-assed. Smoking dope is silly. Getting caught for it is silly-assed. There is never any reason for getting caught doing something silly-assed because there is never any reason to be silly-assed in the first place. Don't do it. We all blunder now and then, but there is no excuse for being silly-assed, and burning that beautiful old building was silly-assed. There was no reason for it to have been burned, which makes the fire silly-assed. What do you call the clown who set the fire? Sorry-assed? Well, it was sure as shit a sorry-assed thing to do. If the Volunteer Fire Department wasn't so good at their job and located just down the hill we might have lost the entire Oliver Hotel complex instead of only one out-building. Maybe now somebody ought to wake up and believe that something weird is going on with that whole Hotel scene. First "The Rock" disappeared; now that building is on the ground and somebody will be crawling around the foundation before the smoke clears, you can bet on that. I wonder if the Police will keep an Officer here twenty-four hours for however long it takes some sorry-assed soul to get so greedy for gold and paranoid of someone else getting there first to take the chance of getting caught? It was a beautiful old barracks, first lived in by the guys who built the Hotel. Man, what a shame! I didn't realize what this place meant to me, even though I lived in it for only a few months, ten years ago. Now it looks like the aftermath of a Boy Scout Jamboree, and for what? Silly-assed, sorry-assed, and such a waste! Seems to sum-it-up pretty well for me. I've got to get out of here and sit on this one for a while. What's next, torch it's clone seventy feet away or maybe go after the Pump House? How crazy is this going to get? Elk walk between those buildings. Where are the Elk going to walk now? Somewhere away from the smell of smoke, that's where. If we're lucky and have a cold Winter then a wet Summer, I wonder if the Elk could be back as soon as next Fall? Can't anybody see how fragile this land is? What do you want, a small chance for a little gold that wouldn't be yours if you did find it or the certainty of a lot of Elk? Wapiti? Any Wapiti at all are worth more than it would take to get a little useless yellow metal, especially when you know that every tree-hugger and Hysterical Society member would want your blood on the ground and your head on a pike in exchange for them. Why do we live here, to have this happen? The *why* rests in clean air and good water and the people who know you by name, and not locking our cabins for a month at a time. That's *why* we live here. We live here for the Elk and the Deer and the Trout swimming a few feet off the front porch. Putting the torch to that place tonight was sick and wrong. All that remains is the fireplace and chimney, a testimonial shrine standing sentinel over the cremated remains lying in the crypt. Didn't anybody think for a minute that it would go unnoticed or that nobody would know what it was about? Evidently somebody didn't. Or did.

*   *   *   *   *

"The Wheel Bar" takes up most of the space in a too-large-for-a-bar building, but where you actually get your drinks is a long, narrow corridor that runs for about thirty feet with the bar on one side and a row of two-foot-square tables against the wall on the other. It gets so crowded in the summer that those tables can accommodate six, and you'd better have a drink before you got there because it might take you that long just to get served, but the actual bar area only takes up about half of the place. The rest is occupied by a pool table, an antique shuffle board, and another three dozen seats around tables for five or eleven people. A stairway goes to the lower bar, but that bar gets used only during the summer because, despite a huge stone fireplace, the downstairs area is just too damned cold in the Winter. The upstairs bar has more than ample room this time of year for everything that could happen except for the CU/Nebraska game or the Super Bowl. Or the burning of a building we all cared about. The Wheel wasn't as loud as it should have been for being this crowded. In fact, it was eerily quiet. People were talking, but everything was being spoken in hushed tones, and nobody was smiling. Not the sort of atmosphere you'd walk into and

38

stay anywhere other than in your own hometown, but I recognized most of the people in there and knew they weren't acting natural. There is always somebody in a bar willing to make an inappropriate comment at the worst possible time, but it wasn't happening here tonight. Truly a sober crowd. Not a good place to go look for a sober crowd this time of night any time of the year, but when a stool opened at the bar I grabbed it without thinking who was on either side of it. Leaning over the bar to get Marlin's attention it struck me why everybody was quiet; they were all doing shots. Slow shots, and is wasn't Peppermint Schnapps, either. Slow, deliberate shots. Not a toast raised in the name of anything, as most late-night toasts tend to be, just slow, murky, dark whiskey sipping. A scary thought, but it some how matched my mood.

"Mister Jimmy, what'll it be? Budweiser?"

"Sounds good, Marlin."

"You smell like smoke. You want to do a shot? Staple's buying a good-bye shot for anyone who watched it burn, and you smell like smoke."

"I didn't see anyone else there that I know. Sure, yeah, give me a Jim Beam, neat. Does everyone else smell like smoke? I know I do, but I can't smell anything else."

"I'm about ready to unplug the smoke alarm. Couple people said they saw you but you were up close and watching the fire, not looking behind you. Said you were hypnotized by it."

"Yeah, I was reliving some memories for the last time, I guess."

"We all were. Everybody in here. That's what these shots are about, 'to keep the memory fresh in our minds', Rich said. Who do you think did it?"

Get the gossip started early, Marlin, because you're the only gossip in a town of gossips who gets paid to do it. One of the few who lends any credibility to his gossip by having been the bartender for twenty years. "I have no idea who did it, but I'll give you five-to-one I know why it went down. Well," I said while lifting the glass toward the old gullet, "here's to the Oliver. She's a Grand Old Lady despite the scars that come with age." I guess the reason I like Beam is the way it burns going down. Any warm whiskey is going to burn on the way down, so you pick the most tolerable burn and

39

live with it, and Beam is my discomfort of choice. What wasn't my discomfort of choice were the looks I saw when I set the shot glass down.

"We haven't been discussing it out loud too much tonight", Marlin twanged. He usually reverted to his native Texas accent only when he was drunk or stupid, but he didn't seem to be either tonight. He seemed to be trying to tell me something, and it didn't take long to figure out that not talking about the fire would be the popular move. It doesn't take much meat on your bones to be bigger than me, and it takes a bit less than that for you to like fighting more than me, so I dummied-up.

"Who'd you say did it?" Marlin, I hope you know that if I answer that it puts you instantly on my side in a fight. "No, you said 'why' ".

"I don't want to get into this tonight too deep, but they were after the gold."

"What gold? There's gold at the Oliver?"

"I thought everybody knew. Two weeks ago I didn't think that anybody knew, and now it's like I took out a bloody billboard." I gave him and the people listening on either side of me a thumb-nail sketch starting when I first worked there and finishing with the missing rock. "So I almost could feel some connection with it except that I haven't told anybody about it for fear of something just like this. It happened anyway, didn't it?"

"Sounds like you know more about it than any other swinging dick in this place."

Ah, Bubba. One shot away from slurring his words, Bubba wants to join the conversation from the antagonist's point of view. I love a rational debate. "How you doing, Brother?" Bubba is one of those five-and-a-half-foot-tall bikers who waddles in at a good 200 pounds, the guy who something in the back of your head tells you not to mess with, and that's why I mess with him. Bikers are an insecure lot, and the only thing you can do about it is give them a sense of security around you. Pull that off, and they'll hurt somebody in your name. That wasn't the idea behind culturing a friendship with Bubba several years ago, but I think that if any trouble ever broke out I'd just as soon have him like me as not. I'm intelligent and well educated, and it shows sometimes. Bikers aren't

40

stupid, just uneducated for the most part, and everyone of them is good at at least one thing so if I can get them talking about it we end up on an even plane. Such was the case with Bubba. "Somebody told me that I'd told him when I first found it, but I don't think so. I told my brother in Arizona, but I also told him why I wasn't telling anybody around here about it, and he concurred."

"Who said he heard it from you?" Marlin never missed many chances to get in the middle of the juicy stuff.

"Some cop out of New York City. I ran onto him last week at the 'Da Vinci'. He got enough of the story right to know what he wasn't talking about and got enough of it wrong to show that he wasn't faking it. I swear I never saw him before, but he knew me by name. He might have grabbed the stone, but I don't think so. He said he'd looked for it and couldn't find it, and I don't think he's had a sudden stroke of luck since then. He might have told someone else, but I don't think so because he'd built almost a passion for it. I have no guess as to who, but I think I know the reason why."

"You're already ahead of us on this one, Jimmy. Lots of people might want to hear that story."

"Lots of people are looking for a whipping boy about now, me included. I'm going to call it a night. See you later, Marlin. Catch you, Bubba." I didn't really expect to get out of there that cleanly, but the somber mood was still the order of the day, and while they were pondering that I made my break.

I don't know if I prefer this town in winter because there aren't so many tourists or because it's just so incredibly beautiful. Snow hanging on the little ledges of the cliffs surrounding the downtown area give a stair-step entrance to town from the outside: "Scramble on in, the living's fine." Climbers come from near and far to test the frozen waterfalls around the valley. Fine time of year for ice climbing. Fine time of year to burn down the town. The last place in town to be burned down will be Delmar's Discount Rocky Mountain Liquor Store. Sounds like some Iranian-owned place where the manager is always choking on a fur ball while he's yelling at the clerk, but in this case it's just a good old boy who retired from the Army and then did anything other than retire. He and his wife Sheryl put too many hours a day into that place, but they wouldn't be there now. Diane would be there now and hers' is one job I wouldn't want to have. She doesn't have to worry about robberies or any of that crap that haunts urban liquor stores, but she always needs to deal with a local without any money who wants a bottle and a six-pack. She always seems to do it with a smile too, which is one of the three most important drawing-cards to shop at Delmar's; you know they're open, the prices are cheap, and Diane will always be smiling. She wasn't smiling tonight, and neither were any of the other larger-than-expected crowd of people in there. I had this sudden urge to come up with a "Space Shuttle Challenger" joke about the Oliver, to be the first kid on his block to make a pure and utter ass of himself, but I think that such an attempt would be best left untested. Grab a half-rack of Bud and one of each Lotto and I'm out of here.

"You smell smoky, Jimmy. What do you think?"

"I think I'm going to go home and try not to dwell on it."

"That car of yours sure looks pretty going down the road."

Bless her heart. Diane always seemed to know when to let you go. Her daughter cuts my hair and seems to share the same trait; when the haircut is over so is the conversation, and it all seems to go so smoothly. I don't have that talent.

I don't often drive through town at night because by the time I usually get off work and into town it's late enough that I have reason to be nervous about the cops. Maybe not tonight, because the two cops who walked through the Wheel didn't get spoken to or reassured by anybody in that special little way that drunks have of assuring the cops that they weren't driving. That's not how you treat the local cops, by snubbing them. You're nice to them and reassure them you're not going to stomp their heads or whatever it is that the local cops want to hear. That isn't the way it was tonight, and I think it may have left them a little shaken. Remove the ass-kissing from the equation and the equation falls apart, and there's not much more than the unknown to set a cop fidgety. I didn't expect to get stopped on the way home, and if I did get stopped I had only sucked-down one Bud and one shot of Beam, but the problem is that in this town there are fewer than one hundred people for every Law Enforcement Officer, and those gentlemen need to justify their existence in a non-crime area while not scaring-off the tourists. God forbid we scare the tourists and put a black smudge on the face of our city fathers. Locals want to live here and seem to be more than tolerant of the antics of the Constabulary, which means that they're a steady source of income for the cops which doesn't slow the flow of tourists, or, more importantly, the Touro-Dollars. For now I just want to wash this smoke off me and have a beer and not get hassled by those two State Troopers parked by the gas station. I'm cool because State Troopers actually have a job to do and a reason to live so they're not going to be interested in me.

Don't see too many State Cops up here this time of year so maybe some poor dumb loser is going to get popped with a couple of quarters of pot. When that happens everybody gets his name in the paper, is awarded citations for bravery and motherhood, and by virtue of being in town The State gets a nice slice of the pie so the Governor may allow himself to take a modest bow. Small town politics in action. Why do they even bother hassling Marijuana? Cocaine, you bet, but Pot? I choose not to use either one, but I've never had an abortion and I have an opinion on that, too. I think they ought to teach kids about drugs in school, and this time make it the truth; if a drug is harmful explain exactly why, and if it's not harmful then the Powers-That-Be should perhaps restructure their ideas toward it. The salaries of the extra teachers needed to teach it could be easily off-set by the Law Enforcement Officers who wouldn't be necessary other than to patrol the alternative. I've always been a dreamer, though, and feel that education should be made as good and accessible as it possibly can be, all heavily subsidized by tax dollars that now go to a fruitless War On Drugs. There can be no better war against ignorance than education, but that message seems to have somehow gotten away from our fearless leaders, Ronald Reagan being the best example that comes to mind. He could have walked on water during his Presidency and I would have had no respect for him because I lived in California while he was Governor there, and if he never did anything else while he held that office, he *quadrupled* the tuition at one of the world's finest systems of higher education. I don't need to get off on that tangent now.

I'm uptight and I shouldn't be for any reason other than that is how I feel. Watching that building burn took its toll on a lot of people, but I don't know why I should be angry. Maybe a little because it somehow doesn't surprise me that it went down, but there was nothing I could have done about it. What would I tell the police, that I thought that somebody would burn a building someday because of a rock I couldn't produce? I don't think so. Forget it. I've got a date with a cold beer and a hot shower and my own warm bed. I don't have a date with the answering machine, so it can wait. I should have snagged that rock the first time I ever saw it and buried the bitch, or at least sent it off to be assayed. Then it wouldn't all be a guess and conjecture as to what is going on. What *is* going on?

* * * * *

I always thought that having a washer and a dryer in the bathroom was a hideous waste of space until I got a place where the washer and dryer were in the bathroom, and then it all made sense. I change my clothes twice a day; once when I get ready for work , and once when I get home from work. On the way to work I'm ready for a shower so the socks and skivvies go into the washer and I'm done with them until I do the next load of clothes. I don't know what the designers of these bathrooms had in mind when they put cupboards over the washer and dryer, but my cupboards hold socks and skivvies. That's where I go to put them on and take them off and to clean them, so why carry them to a different room just to put them away? Makes sense to me. The washer makes a good place to stuff smoke-filled clothes, too. I'll start them as soon as I'm out of the shower, but I don't want competition for the hot water and as good as this feels I may stay here for the rest of my life.

I don't remember when I became addicted to listening to music in the shower. Must have been when I had that day job and listened to those obnoxious clowns on the morning radio out of Denver joking about the traffic and the crime and all the rest of the junk that makes a theirs such a loving community-sort-of-stuff while I showered. Denver has so much love that they want to share some with us. Thanks, but their sort of love has the intimacy of a ten-dollar hooker. Keep your crime and your gangs and your arson. Right now all I'm interested in is what Jimmy Buffet has to say, and since he's saying it and I'm clean again (Clean again! Clean again!..

Good Lord Almighty, I'm clean again!) it just might be time to crack another Bud.

"Telephone."

I had a friend who always answered the phone like that, and in its' own strange way it made a lot of sense, so I adopted it. Every now and then I get a call where the caller asks what I mean by "telephone", and my simple response is to say, "it was the telephone that was ringing so I acknowledged it". If they don't like that I hang up the phone and answer the refrigerator. Something is ringing and I'm unreasonably determined to find out what it is. Either the caller (the person dialing) will return to the callee (the person answering) and get on with it, or I have just had a chuckle at his expense. I try to amuse myself when I can.

"Telephone", I answered again.

"Telephone someone who cares, Jimmy."

"No need to do so as long as you keep putting quarters in the slot", I giggled, sliding the handset smoothly back down into its' cradle. At least now I knew it was Jody, the person who introduced me to the "telephone" guy in the first place. I don't want to talk to Jody tonight; I don't want to talk to anybody. I have four messages on the machine that I haven't played yet and I'm certainly not in the mood for a live audience. He's a persistent little bastard, I'll give him that.

"Yeah, Jody, what's happening?"

"This call has cost me nearly a dollar so far just to get through. Don't you think it's a little rude to keep hanging up on me?"

"I think it's a little rude for me to keep hanging up. I think it's a lot rude for you to keep calling back. What's happening?"

"The Oliver Hotel just burned down!" Jody has this penchant for breaking the news gently, and getting it right the first time. "The whole thing is a pile of ashes."

"When did it happen?" Inquisitive minds want to know, like mine.

"About two or three hours ago. Nobody knows yet if anyone survived. It was horrible," said the man who rarely missed the chance for the theatrical, "oh, the humanity!"

"Have you seen it yet?"

45

"No, I just got back from Denver. She sure is a cow."

I love conversations with Jody. He starts out by telling you whatever it is that he called to say, and invariably finishes the sentence with a social comment about his girlfriend. He has become so predictable in the last few years that I have found that if I don't quickly show some form of solace to the misery he suffers from "that woman" he'll simply wait until I do. I don't answer because their whole relationship reflects that "stupid something" inherent in the dysfunctional magnetism which draws he and his girlfriend so closely together, and I can out-wait him when I'm in the mood to do so..

"Jimmy, what are you going to do about it?"

"Absolutely nothing. She's your cow, not mine."

"I mean the Oliver Hotel! What are you going to do about it?"

"I plan to write to the State Legislature and make it against the law. That ought to deter any arsonist that I know. What would you like me to do about it, Jody?" Not only was Jody one of my oldest and closest friends, he was also one of the most intelligent persons I've ever met. It just wasn't too hard for me to get something past him sometimes.

"I think you ought to do something, or somebody ought to do something. It just burned down, and now it's all gone."

"It isn't all gone, Jody. The South Barracks went down, but every thing else is still there. Where'd you get your information, Panic Central at Our Lady of the Late Night Talk Radio?" I was already tired of listening to him. Well, not him as much as anybody in general. The Wheel hadn't been much fun and I was hoping to cap the night off with myself and the mild buzz that accompanies a couple of beers. "I was there shortly after the fire started. I went by your house toward dark, then took the By-Pass because it's the quickest route to where it was I was going when I saw the commotion. I parked PIGIRON by the knoll and just walked up watching the smoke turn to flame and then to ashes. It was the South Barracks". I remember when the roof started catching fire. Toward the center of each room was the last part to catch flame, and I recall wondering if the suspended light fixtures actually shielded the roof that much or were the flames just flowing in every direction as fast as they could? Is that what you want to hear, Jody? That's how me and a lot of other people saw it happen, and the mood of the town is weird. "You been downtown, yet?"

"No, but I might walk down in a while. Anything you want to know specifically?"

Bless his heart, Jody knew when to cut himself short and get on with the conversation. "I just want to hear what's being said about the fire. I'm off tomorrow, so why don't I meet you at your office around Eleven. Cool. Catch you then."

Today must have been Tuesday. Good thing I get Tuesdays off. I could never seem to get the hang of Tuesdays.

*   *   *   *   *

Jody's office is the Wheel Bar. Every town has a bar named 'The Office" except Estes Park, so that's what Jody calls The Wheel. He refuses to have a phone in his home because he got into an argument with the Phone Company about five years ago and now that he has himself thoroughly convinced that he was absolutely and totally without question 100% wrong in his argument he can't get a phone anyway, so if you want to find Jody try The Wheel first. Jody knows that too, and that's the only reason, according to him, that he stops in there almost every day. His hassle with Ma Bell started out, according to Jody, when he went on vacation and somebody charged long distance calls to his phone. The Phone Company won't allow you to charge calls to your phone if nobody's there so his story already pales in it's validity, and the reason they have that policy is to avoid hassles like this one with Jody. The problem is that he got so much mileage out of the story for so long that to get a phone now would cause him to lose too much face, or, better put, it would cause him to realize that he's already lost too much face. He's already told everybody who would listen that he got the Phone Company to reduce his bill by half and still refuses to get one. It's got to be as obvious to Jody as it is to everyone else that his phone story has, as I said, paled in it's validity, but he doesn't have much of a life so we don't hassle him about it. Too often.

"Mr. Jimmy. What'll it be, a cold Bud or a Bloody Mary this time of day?"

47

Nice to see Marlin back in form. Nice to see Marlin at all. He works days, but was here last night. Double shifts aren't his forte; bets are placed "over/under" on whether or not he'll make a preselected number of hours a week, say, thirty, on his regular shift. Double shift for Marlin? I think not. "Bloody Mary sounds good this morning, thank you sir." It takes about as long for him to build a Bloody Mary as it does for me to take off my jacket and grab a five from my wallet, and I always grab a five because I can never remember how much a Blood Mary costs. I don't think I've ever asked. It's somewhere around $3.00, but if I'm going to worry about it I can't afford to drink it anyway. "What happened last night?"

"Hey, Cousin, you were there. They burned a building up at the Oliver, that's all."

"Who are 'they'? Anybody got a guess?"

"Everybody's got a guess, and no two of them are the same. What do you guess?"

"My guess is that it wasn't a random act. Who ever did it burned that particular building for a reason. It couldn't have been for insurance 'cause I doubt that building could have been valued in excess of a month or two of the back-taxes the new people inherited. Look, the new guy is the ninth or fifteenth owner that place has had since it last turned a dime, which was sometime in the early Fifties. It's been a reverse-money pump for generations. Not saying that somebody didn't try, but Grand Hotels are simply not a destination of choice for too many people since the Interstate System was built by Ike, the last President that wasn't assassinated or impeached. I would think that as the population grows the need for the sort of uncrowded atmosphere that only money can buy would grow with it. I don't think anyone did it for insurance."

"Why don't I wait until you give this some thought, and I'll check back with you", Marlin snickered on his way to serve a shot of Black Jack to a wide short-guy with his back to the light coming through the front window.

I guess I had become occupied with it, but I hadn't realized that I'd thought it out quite that far. I haven't been this drawn-up in anything since the last time I dealt with the Veterans Administration. I eventually just became disgusted with the VA and blew-them off,

48

which is sure what they were expecting me to do because they ride on the train which says there isn't any law against being stupid. Ask *any* Vet about that. This one isn't just going away, though. Then here comes the wide-glide from the sunny end of the bar and while I can't see his eyes, the tilt of his head shows that he's looking at me.

"Jimmy, I'm glad to find you here."

It was the raspy voice that identified him. "Pauli the Pig. You want me to ask what you're doing here or should I just make a wild guess?"

Chapter Five

"You don't have a Chief of Police. You have a game-show host."

"Still trying to win friends and influence people, heh, Pauli?" I wouldn't have guessed that he would have been here, but it didn't surprise me in the least to see him. I don't think anything would surprise me too much right now. "Most people around here think of it along those terms, but I don't believe I've heard it put quite so eloquently. What brought that up?"

"Observation brought the statement. Retirement brought me here."

"You did it that fast? I mean, you mentioned retiring last time you were here, but that was just two weeks ago. This is a nice place and all, but are you sure this is what you want to do? You retired, quit the force?"

"Hell, I made that decision two years ago. It isn't that I don't like being a cop, but I don't want to be the kind of cop I've been since I left the Marines. You in the Marines?"

"Navy, four years as a 'black shoe'."

"Navy puke."

"Slimy Green. How many verses in the Marine Corps Hymn?"

"The Hymn don't have verses. It's 'The Hymn'."

"Beep. Wrong answer.

"Where'd you learn about The Hymn?"

"There are three verses, and it was the first song I ever learned. My father was a Night-Fighter-Pilot for the Marine Corps. He made sure my brothers and I learned that song first.   So now that we both know all about Kiwi Shoe Polish, what brings you back to town?"

"I retired, like I said, and wanted to get out of The City for a while.   Thought I'd stop here and see what was going on, then maybe get a Winnebago and drag that Jag behind it. Make some of the old farts squirm when I blow past them on the road. Maybe start

50

my own personal police force and do it the way I think it should be done."

"Pauli-The-Pig, Inc. Has a certain ring to it. Where do you expect it to fly?"

"Do you have any idea how annoying it is for you to keep referring to me as a 'pig'?"

"No, but I can guess. Do you know how much you irked me calling me 'boy' when I first met you?"

"Yep, and that was on purpose. I wanted to see what you were made of."

"And... ?"

"You're okay. No great shakes, but you have a level head."

"Thanks. I guess."

"That wasn't a compliment. More like an evaluation. I wanted that gold and needed you to pin-point it for me. I still want that gold, and still may need you."

"Evidently you're not the only one who wants that gold. My first best guess is that "the Rock" came from the foundation of the building that went down last night, and as soon as everything gets washed-off we'll go take a look."

"What do you mean, washed-off?"

"There was a lot of water squirted on a lot of burning wood last night. Water and carbon make ink. The foundation has been coated with ink, and the only way to see through the ink will be to wash it off. If you want to find out who started the fire, look for the person with the garden hose and scrub brush. It's still private property, though, and everything I said before still goes. Forget the gold. Catch an arsonist, maybe, but forget that gold."

"You know I'm not going to forget any gold, but I understand what you're saying about it and I've already made plans to back-off on you. I would like to take a look at the site in daylight. You doing anything right now?"

"Other than finishing this Bloody Mary, no." I enjoy a Bud or a Bloody Mary when I have a day off, but usually only one and never more than two. It disjoints the rest of the day too much. "You're not in any hurry, are you?"

"Not any more than a kid wants Christmas. Think we'll have any trouble getting a look?"

"No. I expect the place will be crawling with everybody or completely sealed-off, but there's a seventy-five foot pile of boulders right behind it that gives a great view where we won't be easily seen. So, tell me, you think you can support yourself with a detective agency in Estes Park?"

"No, and I wouldn't even try, although I may apply for a Colorado license. I'll get a pension from New York, but in Estes Park I don't like what I see."

"Nobody likes what happened last night. Were you around last night?"

"Not while it was burning. I got into town about the time the last fire truck left. You got some nice equipment here for a Volunteer Fire Department. They any good?"

"Yeah, they're tops in their class." The only experience I've had in fighting fire was in the Navy. They put me in the back of a concrete building filled with fuel oil about three feet below some deck grating I've got to walk over, get it blazing just right, then tell me it's okay to come out now. Intense, but it's kept me from being afraid of fire. I learned to respect fire a lot, and I respect our volunteers even more. "We freely offer liberal criticism of any and all our honored public servants, but these guys are our neighbors and really put their butts on the line for us. We regard them with a subdued admiration."

"They sure leave your cops in the dust. You can't go into a restaurant without evaluating the waiters, right?"

"Yeah", I said, not wanting to guess what was coming next.

"Same with me and cops. I can't seem to go anywhere and not watch the cops. Take Southern California. Those guys are scared out of their minds. They didn't beat-up Rodney King because he was black or anything else. They whopped him because they were scared out of their minds, and for a good reason. The LAPD patrols seventy-two communities and they are so big and so widespread that the cops not only intimidate the civilians, they've intimidated themselves into thinking that's how you treat civilians because civilians aren't cops and can't understand what the police are going through. Small towns have the other end of the phenomenon. They get so overwhelmed by nothing to do and not knowing how to not do it that they intimidate the locals in order to even a score that doesn't exist. Very stupid way to run things, but unfortunately too common. Your's is a basket case. Like I said, you've got a game-show host in charge of the badges and guns. You know that all but three of the cops on this force were fired from other cop-shops before they found a home here? That means that less than ten percent of your force is fit to serve."

"You have access to the numbers which support that stuff, Pauli. The rest of us just live with it. Ask Jody what he thinks about our Boys In Blue. He knows them pretty well."

Jody had joined us, but Jody joining us means he'll read the Sports Section of the Rocky Mountain News at us until he finds a team he wants to bet on, then he'll go up and down the bar cajoling somebody into risking a dollar. Jody's either a very good or a very bad gambler because he's lousy at picking teams but will only bet with someone who is equally bad, so he breaks about even by the end of the week, and does it one dollar at a time.

"I don't think that Rick or Gene are fools. I don't know many of the others."

"There aren't any others", Pauli cut in. "And from what I see, the town is about tired of it. Shoot a Banker and burn a hotel. Prelude to Watts in '65. It's a comedy of errors and nothing trivial."

"Jimmy, you want another drink?" Marlin was never around when you needed him, sort of like the cops, but he always appeared eventually and asked questions that could easily be left unasked. "Who's your Buddy?"

"No, I think this one will do it for me. I want you to meet Pauli from New York. Marlin, Pauli. Pauli, meet the best bartender in town."

'Marlin, you mix a mean Black Jack. Pleasure to meet you."

"Pauli, the pleasure is mine" returned Marlin, shaking the offered hand. Marlin is a big boy, close to a foot taller than the New York cop, but his hand was almost dwarfed by Pauli's. "You up here on construction?"

"Kinda. I'm sort of into re-constructing. Let me ask you, Marlin, what do you think of the local cops?"

"I love them more every day since I got my DWI. May God Bless Them."

We who work with the public have certain "code words" we use, although we don't all use the same ones. It's a matter of conveying our true feelings in terms the public wants to hear but is afraid to understand. For example, I know a lady who could look you in the eye and blissfully say "God Bless You" and if you looked into her smiling, sparkling face you could see "get fucked" written all over it. That sort of "May God Bless Them".

"Cops stroll through the bar now and then and I don't mind seeing them. It makes for something to talk about after they've gone. If they do take somebody out of here it's generally some clown from the valley up here to make a cheap score on the locals, and we don't consider them much of a loss. Why you interested in this little Burg?"

"It ain't that much little if you stop and take a look at what you've got. There's an over-all population of two hundred thousand, but a year-round population of less than five thousand. What do all those ninety-seven-point-five percent of the 'residents' do for the seven months they ain't here, and what justifies them having the police force they basically pay little to support? Do they expect their lawns to be mown when they get back from Arizona in late April? Who hired these clowns? You could get rid of a third of them, nobody'd know they were gone, and everybody else could get a raise. That would attract better cops and you wouldn't need as many of them. What's left over could go to more teachers, or at least a nice raise for the ones you got, and it would save enough taxes in the long run that the only civilians who'll complain are the ones who'll complain no matter what you do."

"Pauli used to be a Policeman himself", I offered, "and had access to that kind of information. He probed my background pretty good, too." I don't know if I'm still upset about that, but nobody really enjoys being probed, at least not while they're wearing clothes.

"You want to run for Mayor, Pauli? Sounds like you got most of our problems settled for us."

"The problems of a small town are the same as those of a big town, just less red tape to cut through and fewer egos to appease. Come on, guys, this town is going down the tubes like every other town in the whole bloody world, and it ain't because of the Commies

54

or Niggers or Fags. It's because communication has immersed us with information faster than we can absorb it and we're all going out of our rabbit-ass minds because we can't begin to fathom the depth of it. We know what's going on in Bosnia, wherever the Hell that is, and I'll bet you can't even name your Congressman. You don't even know what your Congressman does for a living, but you've both already gone to war once to make sure he keeps on doing it, and if CNN is on their toes you can watch your kids go to war to make sure Bosnia can do it too, wherever the Hell that is."

"I don't have any kids," I broke in, "and I don't give a tinker's damn about Bosnia regardless of how un-American that may sound. And I don't care that much about Estes Politics. If I'd wanted to be a Yuppie I would have used my degree."

"You in denial about anything in particular, or are you just hiding from the world in general?"

One thing I'd learned about Pauli-the-Pig is that I could be up-front with him. I still don't think I could get drunk-enough to figure I could kick his butt, but if he had any respect for you he wasn't going to jump physically. Never would have thought Mickey Spillane would think much about anything other than "Bimbos and Capers". This guy is a trip. Still a pain in the neck, but at least he wasn't always talking about the gold.

"Pauli, I haven't locked my cabin in nearly three years, and if I hear a noise outside it is more likely Elk foraging than anyone screwing around with PIGIRON. You want to call it denial, go ahead. That's a popular buzz-word for someone who wants to disagree but is afraid to be accused of disagreeing. I don't call it denial because I'm not denying anything. I don't deny that there are far too many people on the face of the Earth, I don't deny that there's too much violence tolerated within Society, and I don't deny that our local politics and politicians are licking the 'toe jam' off the foot of our existence. I just don't care. These people will set their moral standards where they will, and they'll go home at night to a hot meal and a warm fire and a cozy bed. That's their deal, and I hope they enjoy the life they're living. I don't want to live an existence comprised of 'Morals of Convenience'. So don't suggest that I'm trying to 'deny' anything, please. Call it avoidance, maybe".

"Morals of Convenience?"

"I don't need the trouble I don't start, and I find that the more I brood on the negative junk the more willing I seem to be to accept it. I don't want to accept it, I don't want to be a part of it, and I have little patience with those who do".

"You ever play spin-the-bottle when you were a kid?" Pauli could change a subject with alarming speed. Maybe that was the New Yorker in him.

"A couple times, but by the time I was old enough to get the nerve to do it, I had other goals on my mind. Why?"

"The point is", he rasped, "that you never knew who it was going to end up on, or how enthusiastic she was going to be." So much for a subject change. "They had to kiss you, but that was the only rule. If the first time you kissed her it wasn't too great, at least you 'broke the ice'. See what I mean?"

"Sure. Yeah. No. Huh?"

"Crime's bottle just landed on Estes Park. Maybe for the first time ever, or maybe for the first time you've ever noticed, but crime is here, boys, and it rarely goes away on it's own. Once you kill a Town Father or torch a building it's like an invitation for others to do the same thing. You've 'broken the ice' for crime."

*   *   *   *   *

"I want you to tell me everything you know about that building, and don't leave out one detail."

We were up in the rocks overlooking the burn, but we weren't hiding anymore than the other nine people up here with us were hiding. The police had sealed the area all right, but the men who were watching the lines were 'Rent-A-Cops', the same ones who herded the tourists in summer. Strange, but stranger yet was that we also found the person with the garden hose and the scrub brush, and it was none other than our own Volunteer Fire Department. Hey, these guys sell us our lumber and rewire our homes, and their bosses turn them loose to save lives and property, not to scrub out the dead foundation of a relic barracks.

"It was used as rooms for the servants of the Hotel guests after the place first opened, then became housing for the college kids who came for the summer work, and I don't think there were two identical rooms in the place. A magnificent stone fireplace facing the main doors, and a stairway to the second floor next to a kitchen that resembled a combat zone. The eleven doors led to rooms altogether different from each other. The closest to the foyer were the sort you would expect to check into in downtown Tijuana, but as you went down the hall they kept getting wider until, on the south-facing, sunny side of the building was a room with a private bath. The occupant of that room was the one who had lived in the building and had worked at the Hotel the longest."

"Tighten the story a little, okay? They've about got it cleaned up and I want to get a good look before they start walking on it."

"From the outside it seemed to make some sort of symmetric sense, but there was no rhyme nor reason for the inside to be set out as it was other than pure hierarchical architecture, and I doubt a building of that sort will ever be built again."

"Close enough. Sounds like the kind of old building I'd like to rummage through. Want to try to get down there yet?"

"May as well. The first person to walk around down there will be the first person to ask, if he asks at the right time. Or not ask and just do it. It isn't like we're criminals."

"That's the answer I was looking for. Let's go down and act like the paparazzi and be as obtrusive as we can. If you can't dazzle them with brilliance, baffle them with bullshit. Trite, but it works."

It didn't work, but Pauli is good at what he does and he was in the process of showing me just how good. He had managed to engage a Rent-A-Cop in what appeared to be a deep and philosophical conversation, although from where I was standing I could only guess at that through the gestures being made until Pauli signaled me over to join him.

"Jimmy, me lad, would ye cast a gaze upon the carnage wrought herein."

An Irish cop? Too deep and too thick for my blood, but if that was the direction he wanted to go I only needed to agree with him and not laugh outloud. Take it away, Pauli!

"Me thinks, Jimmy-Boy, that there is enough scorching upon the side of this edificial foundation to suggest that perhaps an electric

57

lamp hadn't burst upon an upper floor to begin the conflagration. Tell me, Chief, have you suggested arson?"

"I haven't suggested anything, sir, but you can be sure that the people investigating it are the best in their field. I haven't been informed of any of the details of the investigating so far".

"That's what we're all counting on, son, that the best man will do the best job, and the results of his findings could be taken as Sabbath".

That might have been not too deep for the kid, but it was enough to make me turn away in case I laughed.

"Do you have any particular interest in this fire, Sir?" The Rent-A-Cop seemed almost nervous, as though he wouldn't mind talking with anyone but had been told not to. Since the "real" police hadn't been here all day maybe he could justify the conversation with an official-sounding question or two of his own.

"Not just this fire, son. I've investigated quite a few fires and when one occurs such as this it always sparks my interest and makes me want to have a look around."

"Who are you, a Fire Marshall?"

"Not exactly, but I have been brought in occasionally to assist them."

"Do you have any ID, sir?" The Rent-A-Cop was doing just right. He was being a good boy, like his Momma probably said he always was. "I'm not trying to be rude, but nobody is to be admitted to the scene yet. Do you have any ID, sir?"

"Oh, I'm not asking to be admitted, me son. I'd like a look, though, if I may. Just a glance at the pitiful ruins."

I think I see what he's doing; playing "Stupidman" - more power than an Okie-Motive. I'm getting a quick lesson from a pro, and it's coming just before Christmas. What a treat.

"Here's me credentials, Chief, and I hope they match your criteria."

I don't know if cops purchase their badges from the Department the same way they buy their guns, but Pauli had a badge that impressed the Rent-A-Cop to the point in which he was taken-aback. Maybe he'd never seen a real badge before. It was certain that he'd never worn one.

"Let me ask you, son, where the regular Policemen would be?"

"I couldn't tell you, Detective. I got a call yesterday asking me to come up this morning, and I haven't seen a single one since I got here."

"Terrible thing happened here, son." Good move, Pauli; he's calling you by your title and you're calling him "son". The pecking order has been officially established. "Good to have reliable people on the call."

"Thank you, sir, but they always give us a day or two to get here, and this time of year everybody can use a few extra bucks."

It would have been nice to stick around and watch how much more information Pauli could have gotten out of this guy, but the Fire Department suddenly had a real job to do and their angry sirens were keeping no secret about it while the men who had been using the hoses where shutting off the water, disconnecting and re-folding them into the impatient truck. It wasn't significantly farther from the Hotel grounds to the Visitor Center than from the Fire Station, but at the Fire Station the hoses would have already been drained and hung on the trucks and the Volunteers would be driving warm, dry, and rested. Time was being wasted and you could see frustration being vented. Lots of frustrated folks around these parts lately.

*   *   *   *   *

A popular misconception among people who have never been an eye-witness to an explosion is that they are the fabulous projectile-fires produced by the talented FX people in Hollywood. Spectacular, to say the least, and very destructive if given the time needed to burn whatever it is they're trying to burn, but in reality the only thing fire is good for is making more fire. If you've ever seen a film of one of the Navy's Vanguard Missile launches of the late Fifties, you can get an idea of fire-versus-explosion. Most of those launches resulted in absolute disaster which was a shame because the Vanguard was a real Buck Rogers sort of rocket ship and we all wanted it to work because it was so pretty. It didn't work, and the resulting fire filled a concrete bunker with lots of big flames, but had those flames been allowed to explode in the engine of the rocket, a

59

little at a time like they were designed to do, they could have propelled that massive tower into outer space at a speed in excess of 17,000 Miles Per Hour. Instead of that, they did no more than to scorch a little concrete.

In an explosion the gases generated expand real fast for a short distance. In the case of dynamite, the gases expand at a rate of about 40,000 feet per second which translates to just over 27,000 miles per hour. Granted, with the competition for available space from the ambient gasses (read: The air) they don't go very far at all before they slow dramatically, but they don't need to go too far at that speed to create a lot of hate and corruption and making an extremely high pressure area in their immediate surroundings.. Take a close look at picture of a "nuclear device" going off and you get a vivid visual of the effect of expanding gasses; there just seems to instantly "be" a ring of them around where the bomb goes off. That's the destructive part of a bomb. That's what softens the target for anything else that wants to go through it next, like shrapnel or radiation or a SWAT team. The primary purpose of any explosion it is to give birth to the rapid expansion of gasses which do the true destruction. These gasses certainly are hot, superheated in fact, which is what makes them expand at tens of thousands of feet per second and create fire as they go, but you don't see them. Like a tornado. You don't see a tornado, you see the dust and moisture and farm animals and disposable diapers it picks up in it's path while you're making a nose-dive for the storm cellar.

You could see enough dust and moisture billowing around the Visitor's Center that amidst the broken glass and the rest of the carnage was undoubtedly a used Pamper or two. This is, after all, a tourist town. This explosion could be more felt than heard, and more seen than felt. From our vantage point on the knoll above town we could see how it's "Saltbox" roof had opened slightly at the north end but hadn't collapsed entirely into what was left of the building, due in part to the tremendous snow-load capacity of the roof but mostly because the windows had conveniently opened to release the main force of the explosion. Opened in a million places.

"There's a war going on. Have you noticed it yet, Jimmy?"

"I haven't been looking for it, no, but I'd think it will be kind of difficult to disguise it from here on out. Perhaps I should start looking for it just to be able to stay out of it's way."

"Well, you won't have to look very far. All those people who were here five minutes ago have gotten down the hill and about as close to the Visitor Center as they're going to get. The real cops already have their picket lines set. They've sealed the scene, just like here, only now 'here' doesn't seem to count for much anymore, not for the minute. They, whoever is calling the shots, all of a sudden aren't too worried about last night's fire like they were before they got a call telling them when and where the next bomb was going off."

"Pauli, what have you figured out that seems to have eluded me?"

"Let's go look at the evidence we already have. The Rent-A-Cop had at least one day's notice to come up here. That means he was called before the building was burned, which indicates that somebody with the authority to call him had prior knowledge of the crime before the match was lit. Who has that authority? The same people with the authority to call out the firemen to wash it down for them? Also, the firemen started for the Visitor's Center before the explosion, which again indicates a prior knowledge, but that could have been a warning phone call from just about anybody. There weren't any 'real' cops at this scene all day, but the Visitor Center is crawling with them. Sounds like their priorities were set some hours ago and that makes me curious as to when they were warned about he bomb and just what they did to try to find it. I doubt that the "Powers-That-Be" had anything to do with the Visitor's Center because it's for the tourists and tourists are what the "Powers-That-Be" do for a living. More than likely it was retaliation from someone who strongly suspects what I just said; the Town Fathers are deeply involved."

"That just doesn't make sense. The Town Fathers are all wealthy Minor Deities in the town. They don't need to sell dope or burn buildings or anything else illegal."

"You think they're not involved?"

"I think they're involved up to their pencil-thin necks. It just doesn't make any sense, that's all. There are richer people in town than most of them but it isn't the rich people who seem to be target of what's going on. It's the Town that's the target, and the town hasn't done anything other than be a collection of houses and buildings, some now defunct, which have housed the people and their livelihoods. You can't be angry at a town. The people in it, the laws governing it, and maybe the smell of the place, but not the town."

"What do you think makes up a town if not the people and laws and the smell?"

"That's what make up a community. The town is a place where the community lives and works, but the town is innocent of whatever the community does."

"Noble sentiment, Jimmy, noble sentiment, indeed. Also one of the most sickeningly naive things I've heard from an adult in a long time. You make me want to puke with that kind of talk. You're trying to justify burning this building and blowing the Visitor's Center."

"I'm not trying to justify anything. There's no need for any of this to have gone down, and I don't want to think what it could breed. I just wouldn't mind having a simple answer to a complicated question, that's all, and I don't think I need to like any of what's happening while I'm looking for that answer."

"How hard are you looking?"

"Not very damn, Pauli, not very damn at all. All matter is composed of molecules, and all molecules are composed of atoms. Trip one atom on it's way to the Dairy Queen and everything else will fail to fall out of place. If that particular atom could be located and then isolated, then Mary could have her little lamb and all would be right with the world, and the bad atom could be spanked and sent to bed without dessert. It could be an interesting exercise in imaginative speculation but I have little or no desire to pursue it."

"You come up with an answer to that and you'll be able to justify Detroit and Watts and every other town that's ever been wasted in the name of spite. Get this, there is no justification for anything of that sort so stop trying to make a connection because you won't find one."

"So what do we do from here? Should I stick one thumb in my mouth and the other up my ass and when the whistle blows I play 'switch'?"

"Look around us now. They've left us all alone. A few minutes ago there where a bunch of folks who couldn't get close enough, and now they're all gone. Why do you suspect that this site isn't important anymore? They didn't all need to go to the Visitor's Center. The only other person here is the same clown I was pumping before the Visitor's Center became the Visitor's Crater. Why is he still here if not to watch us? Let's let him watch us real close, because if he's watching us close enough he won't necessarily see anything other than us. Let's make a new friend."

I let Pauli take the lead, glancing back down the hill now and then to watch what had developed into a real fire by now. The Volunteers had rigged six pick-up lines into the lake and the diesel engine of the truck that was feeding the three hoses was literally screaming in anger as the wall of water it spawned knocked down the flames with a vengeance. Not long before that fire wouldn't have anywhere to go but out. Pauli hiked back up the rise to where the Rent-A-Cop was leaning against the carcass of the fireplace, alternately watching the fire and glancing at one of us. At least he wasn't being hostile. He was being a good boy. By the time I caught up to them I think Pauli had convinced the 'Good Son' that he was at least half Irish himself.

"Why don't we bustle ourselves to the sight with our friend Stephen?"

Without a hint of hesitation, the younger man lifted the yellow plastic streamer, waved us through, and if I ever figure out what was said to him I might be disappointed.

I don't know much about constructing foundations, but I should have guessed that when the rock was cut out for this one, concrete would have been laid down in it's place. That way, whoever was doing the building would have a known quality for the foundation instead of simply guessing that the rock was solid enough to hold tons of wood and furniture and occupants. Whoever burned it should have known that, too. Once the "ink" had been washed away, the only thing of interest was Early Twentieth-Century Concrete, and enough of it to block everything else from sight.

Chapter Six

"You hear about the Oliver Hotel?"

"Yeah. It's an imposing white edifice perched on the side of a hill above town. It used to have more buildings in it's complex than it does now, but for the most part it's still there. Why?"

"Wise ass. I mean have you heard it's not in receivership anymore?"

"I didn't know it had been, again." The Oliver Hotel goes into receivership about once every two years. Rumor has it that it's part of the program one of the former owners set up for attracting investors. "Back taxes?"

"Yeah, the IRS swooped down on them again, but there's a little different ring to it this time. Seems that the new owners had looked into the financial history of the place and rationally decided to put up only the same amount of money for a down-payment as they'd be able to write-off in taxes should any "hidden costs" suddenly come bobbing to the surface. When the Federal money-boys knocked on the door looking for a contribution what they got was the deed to the hotel, lock-stock-and-barrel. Wouldn't you have loved to see that? The IRS doesn't want a hotel, they want money, and they used the threat of taking the hotel once too often. Now they've got it and I bet there's at least one bureaucrat in Washington who's asshole is puckering-up over it more than just a little somewhat."

"That means it's Federal land now? Outrageous. Wouldn't it be nice to have enough money to sneak-one in on them like that now and then?"

"I guess that's what the former-new owners thought. They evidently found it a lot cheaper and a lot easier to just give it to the Government Agency that wants it the most. Maybe they'll keep first option to buy it back at a later date at a much reduced cost."

"Where'd you get your tidbit of data, Jody?"

"The Office."

The Wheel Bar is definitely the best place to find out what's going on in town. Gossip Central, to be sure, but also an extremely

64

reliable source of hard information. In a town of parking lots, it's easier to walk the three blocks from the offices of the newspaper to the Town Hall than to drive. At least it's faster, and The Wheel is located smack dab between them. Coming or going, it's a good place to stop in either direction. As a result, the best and worst information in town comes from the same place. News like this, however, is generally endorsed as reliable. During other circumstances the fun would be in playing both sides of the reliability angle with equal aplomb and seeing where it might lead you, but right now the social panacea tends toward sane thought. There's a lot of room for sane thought in this town these days. Like giving away a National Historical Place.

There is an obscure set of laws in Colorado which apply to Federal Lands that had once been privately owned. They are usually applied to mining claims that have been abandoned, and to be sure that was why they were written, but because they were never specified as mining laws they have been adopted for general use and have stood the tests of the Courts. Take Crested Butte in the late '60's, back when Crested Butte was still on the rolls as one of Colorado's Ghost Towns. The AMAX Mining corporation had found what it thought to be a moderately rich layer of Molybdenum under a local mountain and had quietly begun to buy surrounding abandoned mining claims as a buffer around the claims they actually wanted. They might have been able to pull it off except that their plans included removing the mountain to get to the ore, and that brought hard feelings from the locals, the locals in a ghost town being you-know-what. Hermits, ski-bums, and rock climbers are also attorneys, geologists, and political scientists, and they poured out of the hills like worms from the belly of a dead horse. The one local bar was doing things like quietly slipping a free beer for each survey stake brought in, but even if it cost AMAX fifteen bucks to reset each stake, it was still the only bar in a ghost town and it couldn't do much more than that. A local church found out that if it established itself one some of the abandoned claims that AMAX hadn't yet bought, it couldn't be moved so long as there were regular meetings being held. That's what they did, too, smack on the side of the hill the mining company wanted to remove. That was the real sort of leg work which came gratis from the locals, and it took them six years to save their mountain, in and out of Court. That was like what's happening today in Estes. The real work was coming from the locals, and everybody, it seemed, wanted in on the action. The problem remained that there wasn't any specific plan to the action, so instead of having one three hundred-person army poised on the brink of battle there were three hundred one-person armies scuttling about with no direction. Maybe it was better like that, this decentralization. No one person subject to the accusational finger for the actions of anyone other than himself. After all, one man's meat is another man's poison. One man's trash is another man's treasure. And one man's mayhem is another man's method of bringing a small town snuggled in a small valley a mile and a half above sea level in the Northern Colorado Rockies to it's knees. Mayhem. Not many other words for it. A town gone berserk. Total Chaos. Mayhem.

*   *   *   *   *

"Mr. Swanson, there's a gentleman here to see you. He says he has an appointment." The Secretary didn't make eye contact with Pauli until Eddie Swanson came out of his office to greet his visitor, but once she was safely hidden behind his protective shadow her veil of courtesy slipped away and the true sheath of the Civil Servant putrefied itself to the surface. Poor Mr. Swanson had been beleaguered by everyone who came to see him for the last three months and she hoped this stranger wasn't going to be another one. Eddie Swanson had dedicated his life to this town and shouldn't be cast-off like an old shirt the first time a sewer backs up. Damn it, he is such a sweet man. And so gentle, usually.

"Thanks for seeing me on such short notice, Mr. Swanson," Pauli said as he stood, holding out his hand. "I'm sure you're a busy man." Busy thinking about a secretary who doesn't worry about safe sex, Pauli guessed to himself. Her change in attitude hadn't slipped passed him.

"Yes, I'm almost too busy these days, what with a few misguided people making a loud misguided noise." If Eddie Swanson was going to pursue any higher political ambitions than his current status of Town Manager he'd need to learn to do it better than that, Pauli noted to himself. "But I'm never too busy to share a

66

few minutes with the folks who count on me." Eddie opened the door to his office and grinned Pauli in.

It was the sort of office one might expect to shelter somebody in Eddie Swanson's position; small, overly lit, and cluttered with the self-aggrandizing artifacts generated when petty tyrants want to impress themselves by thinly disguising their lack of importance. About the only thing in the room out of place amongst the jumble of awards Eddie annually bestowed upon himself was a small wooden pedestal in one corner, a thick-based squat-and-waddy pedestal not quite two feet off the floor. Resting on it's top, so oversized as to create the illusion of a mushroom, was a rock. Not quite a foot square, the only thing about it which distinguished it from any other rough-cut chunk of the Granitic Basalt common to the area was the stripe of quartz running vertically all the way through it, a vein an inch wide, and that vein was almost yellow.

"Quite the piece of stone, isn't it, Mr. ah, um ...."

"Pauli. It's my first name and I like to use it."

"Yes, then, um, Pauli. It was presented to this office by the Historical Society a few months ago. It had a religious significance to the Indians who lived in this valley." You lying moron, thought Eddie's guest. "So, 'Pauli'," continued Eddie while he busied himself straightening the only piece of paper on his desk, "how may I be of service?"

"You already have, Mr. Swanson", then quickly added, "just by seeing me this afternoon." Put a curb on the sarcasm, Pauli, nobody's arrested him yet. "What I mean is that I'm doing an informal study on the political structure of small towns, and just that I was able to call you this morning and see you on the same day impresses me favorably."

"Thank you, Pauli. We always enjoy hearing that our efforts are appreciated."

"I know your time is valuable, Mr. Swanson, so let me not waste it." Pauli hadn't missed that Eddie hadn't offered for him to use Eddie's first name. "You mentioned just now about 'some misguided people'. What's behind that?"

"Oh, nothing really. I don't mean to down-play anything, but with the small amount of crime we have visited upon our town, a

67

few people have mischievously produced a rash of some very odd and highly publicized events lately."

"Like what, if I may ask?"

"You shouldn't bother yourself with that, Pauli. Besides, I thought you wanted to hear about the Town Government."

"Oh, I do, but I'm thinking that if I knew of any 'special' problems the town was having and then heard how they were being handled I could get a better perspective on what I'm looking for."

"Just what are you looking for? Are you a reporter or something?" No sharp edge to the voice, Pauli noted.

"No." Pauli said with a chuckle. "I've always considered myself a 'something', but a reporter isn't it. I may eventually try to get it published, of course, but that would be in a University Press for a Sociology Lecture. Right now I'm simply gathering information and thought that while I'm in town anyway, I may as well ask the most qualified person to tell me what's really going on." Feed an ego, starve a fool; is that how it goes?

With that, Eddie relaxed into his element, lacing his fingers behind his neck and leaning back to prop his feet on the desk. Doesn't he realize that in some cultures displaying the soles of his feet to his guest would be enough justification to get slapped over the back of his chair? Probably never entered his mind. "I don't know that any of these events are related, but they all happened in a short period of time and are all very atypical of the few pranks that usually occur here."

"Please continue, Sir." Yeah, it was "feed an ego".

"It started a few weeks ago with the cold-blooded murder of one of the members of our own Town Council. Death isn't a rare thing here in Estes, in fact for a town this size it could be considered to be an abnormally high number, but it isn't something we publicize for obvious reasons."

"You have a lot of murders here?"

"Goodness no, not murders, just deaths."

"How do you have 'just a death'?"

"That's actually quite simple, if you'd care to stop and think about it." (Getting a little protective about our town, are we, Mr. Swanson?) "With our proximity to the National Park, there are an almost predictable number of people who come here every year to commit suicide. It's generally assumed that they want to die at above 12,000 feet in order to be 'closer to God' when they go. That accounts for about a third of the people who die here, but neither 'The Town' nor 'The Park' want it advertised for the sake of unfavorable publicity. You understand, of course."

"Of course. You mentioned an abnormally high number of deaths. What accounts for the other two thirds of them?"

"Well, aside from normal civil attrition, you must realize that this is viewed by some not as a tourist town but as a summer home for the retired. We get blue-hairs dropping like flies."

"But few murders?"

"Virtually none."

"That's a rare statistic, but a nice one to have. How is the investigation coming along?"

"It's being kept confidential for the moment. I'm not involved in it so they won't even tell me. I guess they know what they're doing, though, and I ... excuse me." His phone had just began to ring and Eddie already had his hand on the receiver. Almost as if he'd been expecting it to ring.

Pauli stood quickly and opened the door. The secretary's face reddened a little when she saw him, then she whispered a few more words into her telephone, set it back into it's cradle, and looked almost everywhere but at Pauli. How much time, he wondered, had been preordained for his visit? Was it exactly five minutes, or had they been clever and made it something like four minutes and thirty five seconds before she was to interrupt with the call? He turned around to face Swanson, who was still speaking into the handset. "Thank you for your time, Mr. Swanson", said Pauli, knowing he wasn't interrupting anything. "Maybe we can get together again and finish the talk." With that he was gone, leaving Eddie Swanson to finish his mythical conversation.

*   *   *   *   *

Everyone has one or another form of religion, although it is painfully obvious that some wear them more gracefully than others. Religion is defined in Webster's first as a belief in God or gods, and second as a set of beliefs in general. It is my belief to God that religion is so *very* personal that it should be kept to yourself whether you're in an airport or shopping mall or anywhere other than by yourself. If you want to make religion your life, great; there are worse things to be done with a person's mortality, but I like to think I have a life of my own so you keep yours and I'll keep mine and ne'er the twain shall meet. As a result of this conviction, I tend to be quite intolerant to the pleas of Churches for public donations (pronounced "money") to further their Cause. So Churches can watch out for themselves and if a friend of mine is in need I'll go to the wall for him and eliminate the cost of the middle man in the process. I have two good friends who are "Jesus Freaks", albeit benign "Jesus Freaks" in that they keep their thoughts to themselves, and I correspond several times a year with a Maryknoll Missionary, but none of these people have established themselves as "keepers of the World's faith", and to this end I have been able to enjoy their intellectual companionship. That is what I refer to as being "bright" about your religion. Being "bright" by not being offensive to your friends but still allowing your faith to assist you with your life.

The actions of the members of The Church Of The Presumptuous Assumption could be taken in many ways, but "bright" was not one of them. To set an altar in the middle of a burned-out foundation of a building to which a murder could be loosely associated was not "bright" in anyone's book, but embracing the law about Abandoned Federal Lands, that's what they did. They also set a huge tent around it to shield it and themselves from the elements, which it did so long as "the elements" didn't include the air temperature because there was no way that canvas was going to keep either heat in or cold out. But there it was and there they were, and so long as they held "regular meetings" they couldn't be run-off the now-Federal land. That was the law. The Big Law, the law that the Town Council of Estes Park couldn't touch. The term "regular meetings" was no more nor less defined than "prudent man" was defined, but at least those definitions shared any lack of interpretation by all government agencies equally, an unintentional convenience to the public brought about by bureaucratic bungling. It would seem that if the separate agencies would even talk to each other now and then they could not only operate more efficiently within themselves but they might actually achieve the higher goal of making everything else run just a little smoother. Thank God *that* will never happen. So they have their little church on a little chunk of Federal Land from which they can't be moved, and the end result is that presumably nobody is going to try to break-up a concrete foundation while The Reverend Simms and his flock are sleeping on it. The Japanese lanterns decorating the outside of the tent could be said to be in poor taste but religion has never been accountable to "taste", and they did add a festive air to what was an otherwise dark situation.

  The Reverend Antoine Simms had been in town for several years, ministering to a small group of changing faces who joined him in the living room of his modest mobile home on Sunday mornings. Being a realist as well as an evangelist, Simms' meetings were held several hours later than traditional services in the hope that more of his flock would have slept-off that fine line which separates Saturday night from Sunday morning. He would also have a few extra eggs scrambled for the first few to arrive, and on those particularly treacherous Sundays found late in Winter when cabin fever has taken it's toll he has been known to supplicate from the stove while all of his flock got fed. He also took donations, but made no qualms about keeping his day-job in order to pay for the groceries. And the rent. His was not a wealthy congregation, but they showed up at his door on a more-or-less regular basis and that was his great satisfaction. They came because they wanted to come, not because God needed them to come or their collective conscious bade them attend, which, in itself, is a unique situation for a church. They came for breakfast and a cup or two of the "sacramental java", as it had become known to it's parishioners. And they came to worship, to pour-out their souls in song, to relieve terminal hangovers. They came for whatever reasons, but they came to hear The Reverend Antoine when they would not attend any other services, and that didn't endear their Pastor to any of the Mainline Clergy. They wouldn't have been jealous of his flock because this "flock" was the sort which often smelled like one and tested the true measure of Christianity's love of fellow man. They wouldn't have been jealous of their donations because this was the sort of flock that often took more than they gave. The jealousy, if that's what it was, lay in the idea that Simms

71

had gotten them to attend at all; an act which had always eluded the other churches.

Whatever it was, he hadn't found his name on the Ecumenical Dean's List of late, which may or may not have made anybody happy but there weren't too many folks expecting it to be there, certainly not The Rev. Simms. He was happy with his little group of people. He was happy with his little life. He was happy that he was able to bring a little of what he called "the message" to those who chose to hear it and he didn't give a hoot if anyone wanted to say he had bribed them into coming around. Maybe some of the doomspeaks would do well to emulate a few of his methods and watch what could happen to the morale if not the size of their congregations. Rev. Simms had seen what it had done to his congregation, and that was good enough; it made him happy. It also made his living room very crowded, not only on a Sunday morning/afternoon, but people just started dropping by at any time of day or night for whatever reason. Some brought joy, some brought sorrow, some brought drink (maybe a sip), and it was keeping him from much time to himself. His living room, was, after all, his living room, though, and while he welcomed them into his home and his heart, he wouldn't mind finding another place to do it. To this end, available property combined with a sure-fire method of doing a little "in your face" to the high-power high-collars was almost too much to ask for. Thank you, Jesus, thank you, Little Lamb of the Flock.

*   *   *   *   *

David Engleman moved onto the Oliver property the same morning as the Church, but, then, David Engleman was never a man to miss many opportunities to move anywhere with Whitey paying the mortgage. More power to him and to his people. David Engleman was where he wasn't sure he was supposed to be, and David Engleman, to look at his crystal-blue eyes and his wavy black hair, was not Jewish. He could have been, as seriously as he took any religion, but David's father had felt the sharp bite of prejudice one too many times to continue his traditional family name of Eagleman and opted for the name of a man who was once the

72

Superintendent of his Tribal Schools. It still brought prejudice, but this one was nothing he couldn't handle with his eyes closed after what he'd endured. David had jumped on this particular Federal Band-Wagon as soon as he'd found it was available. Not surprising, though, because David was known to jump on about any band-wagon he could, so long as it didn't cost him much. David was also known to jump into a lot of things that weren't Federal, such as the crawl space under a house where he knew that a space heater was keeping the pipes from freezing. Last winter I started keeping a couple cans of Bud in my crawlspace alongside a pallet that held my spare sleeping bag and have found it easier to tell when he's been around by checking for empties than waiting for a knock on the door. Crumbs for Hansel and Gretel. The pallet is covered with a sheet of plastic to keep the dust off, and I don't think that dusty plastic will be fluffed for a while.

Where David got the name "Tony" is one of those things that is none of my business nor any of my interest, but most people around town know him as Tony. So Tony and his dog had set-up camp on the front lawn of what at one time was called "The Gem of the Rockies", and he looked like he wanted to stick around for a while. Complete with a Tipi and a clan that he probably hadn't even met before this morning, what mattered now was that he and the others be seen, and they were being seen. Like what had happened at Alcatraz. When that Federal prison was closed it became "Federal-Land-Abandoned". A mangy group of Indians moved onto it in a loud rebellious manner guaranteed to alienate everybody, then claimed it under laws not dissimilar to the laws set in Colorado. Of course, nobody really ever gave a second thought to Alcatraz. The flip of a switch and the twist of a valve took not only the electricity and the water out of that picture, but the interest of The Public, too. Soon thereafter the Indians went away, although nobody remembers just when because, as I said, nobody really gave a second thought to Alcatraz. The precedence is the same, though; if the Federal Government relinquishes administration of any of it's lands or holdings, those lands or holdings are up for grabs to any of a select group of otherwise federally-abused recipients. Being one-half Native American, Tony could do nothing other than claim this land in the name of his people and his dog. He owed it to them as much as he owed it to himself, at least that was his story, and he was sticking to it.

"Tony, my brother, my heart gladdens at the sight of your face". We didn't play 'Cowboys and Indians' with each other in any way except as a game, but we did play it. It's a great game if kept in the right perspective. "Forsooth, my friend, what light through yonder window, and the rest of it?"

"These acres are mine! We live here now, my people and me! We shall set our ancients' souls to rest as was due them so long ago! After a hundred years we are once more free to right the grievous wrong and roam our lands again. Rejoice! A grave injustice is about to be undone!"

"Cool it, Tony, it's me, and the only roaming you're going to do is from here to the closest latrine, soon as somebody digs one."

"I could dig one before long, if you catch my meaning, if you get my drift. Glad you could make it to the party, but I didn't see if someone else made it here with you. Got to keep it on a level keel, mate."

"Mate? Good talk for a war-hoop."

"You know that if my people heard you speaking to me that way they would have your scalp?"

"You're speaking in metaphors, and I hesitate to think what 'your people' would think of that."

"I be a bidnessman set out to do my bidness. We bein' close to Nature, uh-huh!"

"Wrong accent again."

"Forget that. They're here for the party as much as I am, but we need to maintain some sort of reality, don't we?" Tony is one of those few folks you want to have cross your path just once in your life for the twinkle in his eye if nothing else.

The "reality" Tony mentioned consisted of a ragged tipi, an aluminium lawn chair, a half dozen Native Americans, and two dogs. Three of the Native Americans were sharing a jug of wine, one was asleep in the chair, one was applying war-paint, and one was talking to me. The two dogs were walking in circles smelling each other's private parts.

"Where'd you get the tent?"

"Don't call it a 'tent'. Tents are where you Yuppies keep your Gore-Tex sleeping bags while you're stomping the wildflowers in designer leiderhosen. This is a 'tipi', the traditional home of my nomadic People, and this classic example of Native American Architecture sprang to life when my Uncle got divorced and needed a place to live. It's been in my mother's garage for a few years and shows it, but we're trying to scare-up a few more around town."

"You all going to stay in there together?"

"Far as anybody is going to know. Indian brothers, and all that."

"Sounds good to me, Tony. Hold that story line as long as you can, 'cause you're going to need everything you can muster to pull this off. By the way, just what is it you're trying to pull off? You really plan on staying here for awhile?"

"I don't know. Stay on some real estate long enough to embarrass Whitey. You embarrassed yet? We just got here ourselves, and I don't think anybody really knows we're here yet. I know we plan on making some noise, maybe even joining that church over there 'cause it looks like we're all doing sort of the same thing, you know, locking-up the land. We'll leave the shooting to you cowboys, but we think we're legal and we'll find out for sure when a little more research gets done. That guy with the war paint is a lawyer trying to make an impact in the name of his Tribe, and he's got his staff on it. He seems to think we could stay here forever, or at least until somebody buys the hotel from the IRS. The official word we plan on putting out is that we'll be here 'forever and a day', but we figure we're good for a couple of months, anyway. I don't see why I can't stick around with them for the Winter as long as Po' doesn't get arrested too often."

"Po'" was a dog, and that's about the best one could say for her. Some people tried to guess her breed, but nobody ever got it quite right because that dog didn't have a breed. No self-respecting breed would let Po' in the back door, so she was just Po'. "Poor Dog" was the first thing most people thought when they saw her for the first time, and the name stuck in the abbreviated version. But Po' was a lovable dog if nothing else, which translated into Po' being a lovable dog because that was all she had going for her. Maybe she could be called a "rock-toting dog", because that's what

75

she did best. Not big rocks, like one the size of a fist, which would be too big for a forty-pound dog to run with and comfortably tote, but rocks more the size of an egg were Po's speed. And carry them she would. If I thought empty Budweiser cans under the house were a good way of keeping track of Tony, soggy egg-sized rocks by the front stoop were a dead give-away because Po's was always with Tony when she wasn't stashed securely somewhere else, like dogie-jail. She went to jail relatively often, like whenever the Dog Catcher could get her hands on Po'. Whenever Po' went to jail she was actually doing time for Tony; the cops were putting Tony in jail by proxy, the irony of which was that Po' wasn't really Tony's dog. Po' had come into town with a former roommate of Tony but Po', like so many dogs and cars and children, was seen as a possession of the owner and not valued as anything more. Tony used to take her on walks with him and when anybody began to 'admire' her, Tony would offer to sell her for five dollars. Must have made the offer to me a half-dozen times, but he never got any takers.

"How you set for groceries, other than the Dago Red?"

"There you go again, insulting the other side of my family."

"Say the word 'Honky'."

"Honky."

"Now, how you set for groceries?"

"A might scarce, as you could imagine. We got here on short notice and the wine was sort of just around when we got here."

"And if we're going to be smart it'll be here when we're gone." He-Who-Paints-His-Face had joined us, still daubing-on a touch of theatrical grease paint. "Who's you friend?", he asked Tony while looking me straight in the eye. His grease paint struck me as not the only thing about him that was theatrical.

"His name is Tony, and I think he's part of your troupe." I figured that if he was going to try to intimidate me without knowing me I wasn't going to worry too much about the friendship angle.

"I was talking to Tony."

"You were looking at me. Sorry if I misunderstood. My name is Jimmy."

Okay, he can take a joke. "I'm John Chism, and don't ask." The grin spreading across his face matched his firm handshake, and sometimes that's good enough. "We could stand to stock in some

76

staples just to look like we're planning on staying a while. We can make all the speeches we need to make and dance through the courts 'till the cows come home, but initial appearances count for a lot."

"Let's roast an Elk. We're Indians, and it's our tradition as well as our right!" There were times when Tony could hit the nail on the head, and there were times when he could smash his thumb.

"Why not just make a run on your own?"

"I'd appreciate being able to do that but there's an unknown in our situation that makes me not want to shake the tree before I know if it's going to rain peaches or Feds. I don't know yet what it might take to represent a 'bona fide' Tribe, but there could be a long reach between having six of us here and having only five, and I'd hate to have the odd-man-out at the wrong time."

"Want me to drive down for you?"

Why did I just say that? Maybe because Po' had just balanced a soggy rock on the toe of my left shoe. I don't want to get involved with anyone's cause, but I have some free time and it seemed like what he was fishing for and I like this guy's display of his gonads. It could give me good conversation-fodder for work, and anyway this is getting thick enough that I don't want to miss what I could see from the periphery.

"You sure you wouldn't mind?" John Chism was striking me as one of those intellects I might not agree with but it could be interesting to talk with him.

"Why not? Fuck it, sure." Sometimes a man needs to get right to the point.

"Okay. Before we set-up camp I arranged a voucher at the grocery store in the Tribe's name. My signature is on their list and you need to give them this ID Card when you sign for everything. I told them to expect you."

"Me? By name? I doubt it." The forlorn look Po' was giving me indicated that she was doubting it, too.

"No, really. Tony gave me a list of some people in town he could trust and who might show up, and you're one of them. I put you on the grocery store's list with the others."

"Cool. Now I'm on a list which has probably already been subpoenaed by the locals, and all I wanted to do was take a look around. Thanks, but nothing personal if I ask you to buy your own groceries?"

"Don't worry about it. I added to the list the names of the Mayor and the Chief of Police. I'm a Land-Shark, remember? I didn't see this coming in Estes but I imagined it happening somewhere and have spent many hours after work amusing myself with the scenario. I don't claim to have all the answers yet but at least I have thought it out this far and you can't be arrested or charged with anything for buying food and signing your name. You may get hassled, but not any more than any of the other respected citizens of our town. You're not on any spot, Jimmy, and I won't hold it against you if you choose to not buy a few grits for the Indians."

"Let me ask, if only to justify my own curiosity. When you asked me my name, you already knew it?"

"Yeah."

"How?"

"There's this thing called NCIC, which is a system used by law enforcement agencies ..."

"I know about it. I got introduced to it a month ago, and I'm beginning to think it's on a party-line."

"Very near is. You got a Fax-Modem?"

"Just installed one, but I'm not hooked-up to any BBS yet."

"You don't need to be. All you need is the phone number and access code."

"Want to trade some groceries for an access code?" I didn't have the slightest notion what I'd do with it, but if I could find out what Ronald Reagan's Social Security number is I might get creative.

"Not a chance, even if I had it, which I don't. Some raspy-voiced cop punched-it up for me and then had the audacity to check for an automatic back-up in my system."

"He find one?"

"Even had the nerve to override it", he laughed. "Tony pointed you out to me when you were parking your car so I had a face to go with the name, but I needed to know how straight that face would be with me."

"Like as straight as you are with me?"

"I'm being straight with you, and you don't need to cover your ass every time you turn around. Okay?"

"Okay. You have a shopping list for me?"

"Wrote it over a year ago, right out of the U. S. Geological Survey's *Pamphlet on Provisions for Prospectors*", and bless their hearts for preparing it for me. I would have gotten it all wrong on my own, and with their own recommendations for provisions as a guide the Feds can't very well tell us we're not stocking the right things for an extended stay."

List in hand, I drove down the hill. In a small town grocery store in prospecting country it isn't difficult to find fifty-pound sacks of beans and rice, but here in Estes a fifty pound bag of nearly anything has to be bought five pounds at a time. No big deal, but by the time I had the list filled I was feeling more than a little conspicuous. My shopping cart looked like what a large family might buy the day before the Food Stamps ran out, but, since essentially that was what I was doing although I was doing it for someone else's family, I found a macabre humor in the looks I was getting. I was having just enough fun with this that I almost went to the Express Lane with the overloaded cart, but I do draw the line at being rude.

There were some places and some people in town who could not or would not participate in the local hassles. McDonald's, for example, continued to smile at everyone and if there were any feelings pro or con to what was going on in town on the part of the employees of McDonald's, they were kept strictly apart from the name of the burger chain. As well they should be, and for several reasons. First and foremost, McDonald's is not a corporation given to lending it's name to violent revolution. Social revolution, in the scope of spreading the word of the importance of close family values and going so far as to not only coming to the aid of families in need but establishing the "Ronald McDonald House" as a shelter for those who needed to be near hospitals who could not otherwise afford to do so. They also were doing a lot to keep not only both sides of the fence fed, but there were a lot of moms with cars full of kids who wanted nothing more than Happy Meals with no strings attached and had nothing to do with the fracas, whether they knew it or not. I picked up six Happy Meals from the drive-thru window on my way

79

back to the camp because from what I saw of their organization, those guys would need something to eat before dinner was ready. Maybe I can look at it as a donation in lieu of UNICEF this year. Maybe I can look at it as benign support to a faction that at least has the guts to stand out in public while quietly doing their thing. Maybe I can look at the shoulder of the road while the blue and red lights flashing in my mirrors tell me it's time to pull over before I want to.

My license and registration are always in order because it is so simple to keep them that way that it would be "silly-assed" to be busted for not doing so. Insuring a car the age of PIGIRON is so embarrassingly cheap that I can keep comprehensive coverage on it for less than a hundred a year, and I haven't been to "The Wheel" today so I have nothing to sweat, right? I don't recognize the cop walking toward me, but I couldn't recognize most of them anyway. It was easy to get the formalities out of the way, and then I tried something an Attorney once told me to do. I asked him why he stopped me. Simple as it seems, a direct question which makes sense and is within your rights to ask will usually throw a non-justified bust for a loop.

"I saw you leaving the grocery store ." Snappy retort, Officer.

"And?"

"Would you please open your trunk, Sir?"

"Why?"

Predictably, he made a one-finger adjustment of those stupid sunglasses that only cops wear to shove them higher up that stupid piggy nose that only cops seem to grow and, sticking his thumbs in his thick belt, said, "If you ain't got nothing to hide you shouldn't mind me having a look". He kind of smiled then, maybe because was so proud that he'd remembered all the words he was told to say.

"No problem, Officer. Just as soon as I look in your wallet."

"My wallet is none of your business."

"Neither is my trunk any of your business, but if you ain't got nothing to hide you shouldn't mind me having a look."

Nothing will irritate a cop as much as making sense at them, especially when you're right. Asking them, after they pose an especially stupid question to you, if they're on drugs, can bring them to an unreasonably non-civil frame of mind, but to be safe and still get their goat (not to be confused with their "pig"), you need only make sense. Small town cops are not trained for it, they don't understand it, and it will put them on the defensive. From that point on be polite and cool, and they will likely let you go before they figure out why. Pauli-the-Pig had told me that, and so far it was working.

"Will there be anything else. Officer?"

He begrudgingly returned my documents to me, and they were hardly in the glove box before I started on my way up the hill.

I was not more than fifty feet away when his lights and siren once more became more of a part of my life than I had hoped.

"You saw my "Important Papers" less than five minutes ago, so let's dispense with the formalities. What do you want?"

"You didn't use your turn signal when you pulled away from the curb, and don't try to get smart on me this time, boy."

Boy? You just touched a nerve, Buford. "Well, I guess you got me now, Sir, and every law-breaking, slip-sliding, criminal element needs to be brought to justice. I hope you write the biggest ticket you can write, but make sure you write your name and badge number clearly so that everyone knows who it was that just caught this alleged scoff-law and nipped his crime wave in the bud."

There aren't too many things scarier than a cop who can't figure out why he should be nervous but is anyway, and this reject was a shining example. My ass-was-grass by now because you don't drive a car like this around a small town while playing games with the Constabulary and not carry a high profile, so I may as well make the most of it. If push came to shove, I'd eventually be dealing with cooler heads than his anyway.

"You were right in pulling me over, and that guy on the hill with the binoculars will testify to it. He's your witless. I didn't use my turn signals, and the other guy up there has it on video. You got me. 'I have the right to remain silent, I have the right to an Attorney ...'."

"Shut up, punk, or you're going to make my day!"

Kind of fired-up for a short little fat fucker, ain't he? My Turn. "Look, Buddy, in 1948 turn signals were an option on the

81

Plymouth Super Deluxe, and if you have a problem with that the fault lies not with me but with the people who allowed this car to be licensed in the first place." Man, was I digging a hole for myself. "Go arrest the State Of Colorado, but get off my back. Like I said, it's on video and that should stand up in court, just like with Rodney King. You have a case, so you pursue it. I have some food, and I'm going to deliver it."

I sincerely wish that such a poor dumb clueless bastard as he with whom I had so recently dealt will never find a justifiable reason for pulling me over again, or it's "Good-bye, Estes", and "Hello, Canyon City". I hope Po' likes beans.

Chapter Seven

The Town Council holds it's meetings in the largest room of the Municipal Building because, they claim, they need to be sure there is room for everyone wishing to attend. To that end, all but a very few of their meetings could be held in the Men's toilet, but this is the room they wanted and except on Election Day nobody else ever used it anyway. Tonight was a little different. It was an impromptu meeting and not even the Mayor had been told about it. Perhaps everyone had assumed that somebody else would have told him, which made his absence an innocent act of omission, but it was a shame he couldn't be here to witness the debacle. He has a great sense of humor and would have appreciated it.

The Mayor-Pro-Tem calmly stood, placed his hands palm-down on the table between himself and everyone else in the room, leaned forward and offered them a parable. "There is an empty chair in this room tonight," he said with an air of solemnity, nodding toward John Loughlin's yet-to-be-filled seat, "which is a mute testimony to the turmoil facing this town. We must", he added with a slap on the table, "get to the root of whatever is agitating those few of our citizens who are making such a loud noise."

"That shouldn't be too hard to do," offered a Southern-accented voice from the rear. "All you have to do is take a look around you. The Citizens are talking real angry and scared, and the Cops are now driving around two to a car. With shotguns."

"That sounds like you're trying to get personal, Sir. I don't know how you do it in wherever it is you're from but that is not how we conduct meetings in this town."

"I'm not the one who does it in wherever it is I'm from, so I don't know neither", the voice drawled. "What I do know is that there is nothing 'personal' going on here, not in what I'm saying or the way this town is being administered."

"You think that there's nothing personal in the administration of this town?" This was going to be too easy, thought Eddie to himself. The "outsiders" always thought they knew all the answers.

"With the exception of our two new members," he said, taking the time to acknowledge the man and woman to his left who had just won their seats in the last election. John Loughlin had also won his seat again, but that didn't matter much any more. "With the exception of our two new members," he repeated for the benefit of nobody in particular, "you are looking at over six decades of town administration sitting at this table, and if that's not 'personal', you tell me what is." That should sit him down and shut him up.

"Mr. Swanson, I'm not denigrating the service you and you colleagues have given to your town. More towns could benefit from such dedication."

That didn't take very long to get him back-peddling, thought Eddie. He keeps this up and I might not need to say another word all night.

"But this is a one-industry town," the interrupter continued, "yet not one member of this Council works in a tourist-related capacity. Not only is there not one shop or restaurant or public washroom owned by anyone on the Council, I'd be willing to bet you haven't spoken to the people to whom you owe your tax-base in a long time."

"We don't need to know how to build a clock in order to tell the time," Eddie Swanson chided, "and we can see better than you what's going on in the town." Who did this guy think he was to question them?

"When was the last time you actually stood across the counter from a shop owner and listened, actually listened, to what he had to say?"

"We hear complaints all the time, believe me."

"I believe you, but what do you do about them? You don't represent the shop owners of this town and you don't represent the one industry they provide. You represent a ledger book, a spreadsheet, big numbers on a little piece of paper. So long as your books balance and the numbers grow steadily every year, you think you've done your job. But not you nor any other member of this council has a personal interest in the town or it's people. That is what I mean when I use the word 'personal', and it is the root of the problem that needs fixing, and it needs fixing fast." He was nearly out of breath when he retook his seat.

"Quite an eloquent statement from a visitor, a non-resident. I must pause and ask myself if this stranger has any more suggestions for us before he goes back home?" Eddie was getting on-edge, and his intentional sarcasm reflected it. He was beginning to regret that he'd allowed this to be an "open" meeting.

"I think he's made a very strong point." The "Lady" Council member had never before spoken at a meeting. Helen Brumett had only taken her chair less than a month earlier and she hadn't really been given the opportunity to speak. Even her little speech when she was sworn-in to the office seemed to have been clipped. "I must admit that I hadn't given it much thought until now, but maybe he's right in saying there hasn't been much thought given to a lot of things around here."

"You'll be given the chance to speak when you're 'recognized' by the Council, Miss Brumett." Who's side is she on, anyway? "In the meantime, if you think someone else can do your job better than you, you may always resign."

She might have leapt at the chance to say something in rebuttal, but Ace Palmer was sitting in the front row and beat her to it.

"I recognize her", he said sharply as he stood. "I voted for her, so I damned-well better recognize her. And you, Eddie Swanson, had best curb your bullying tactics right now. If you had spoken to my wife like that I'd rip-off your head and spit down your neck!"

"I insist that this meeting come to order!" Eddie was losing control, something he'd never gotten used to doing.

"You want this meeting to come to order? Stop sniping it's members!"

"Shut up, Mr. Palmer, and take your seat!

"You may not have noticed it, Eddie," Ace continued, "but your tax-base is coming apart even faster than you are, and none of this is doing any of us any good!"

A true money pump should be neither scorned nor taken lightly, and those who wouldn't or couldn't accept that fact needed to be reeducated about the facts of life or taken out of the way. Eddie got ahold of himself for a moment. "Did anyone here expect such a radical reaction to the passing of the 'Low Stakes Gambling Act'?"

That little jewel had been proposed and written by John Loughlin, or, at least now that he was dead the other Council members said it was, and it's lack of popularity rests on his Tombstone. The Mayor-Pro-Tem, who spent over fifty years in Estes being called Eddie by everyone until his recent electoral victory made it more appropriate to become "Mr. Swanson", didn't really care what the Town thought of the Gambling Act. That it was he who had written it, over the objections of the late Mr. Loughlin, was going to be his little secret. He had met Loughlin's objections with the argument that he didn't expect it to pass but he wanted to get the Public thinking that some form of Gambling was inevitable. Look what it had done for the economies of Central City and Blackhawk. When a new but much more subdued Gambling Act would be proposed next year, it could be promoted on the idea that the valiant Counsel Members had found many ways of saving everybody lots of trouble, which would make them heros and ensure the passing of the new law. But the first Gambling Act had passed, due solely to the creative wording designed to confuse the voters, and now that Loughlin was dead the blame had been smoothly transferred to him as an act of devious convenience.

"Radical reaction? It's more like violent hysteria, and I think it's a good Goddamned thing we don't have a South Central area in this town or the Los Angeles riots might start to look tame."

"Mr. Palmer, you and everyone else in the community are always welcome to attend these meetings, but I'm going to ask that responses be restricted to Members of the Council until we schedule a regular meeting. And please watch your language, Sir."

"My language has nothing to do with it. That Act is illegal, and you'd better get it off the books right quick if you want this town to stay on the map." Ace Palmer had come to town from somewhere in the Deep South over forty years ago with, as he'd been know to confide, nothing but a tool belt and a hard-on. Specifically why he left the Deep South has been a point of speculation in the town that he considered to be his own business, but this is the sort of town where not a lot of questions are asked lest the person doing the asking be obliged to answer the same questions. Honest to a fault, he now personally owned more rental units and various vacant lands in and around town than any other single person. He'd literally made millions by pounding nails and digging ditches, and while he lived in an exceptionally modest home and kept his wealth to himself, his opinions were something he'd share with anyone.

"Mr. Palmer," (Eddie Swanson was the only person who didn't call Ace by his first name. Perhaps it was a self imposed and justifiable intimidation on Eddie's part.) "Mr. Palmer, are you threatening this counsel?"

"Eddie, if you'd take the time to listen to your own words you'd see that this Council is threatening itself, but I don't suppose you'd know why a Jack-Ass isn't called a Jack-Genius, either."

"Mr. Palmer, I have asked you once to keep your comments to yourself until a regular meeting, and if you do not comply with that request immediately I shall ask that you be removed from the room!"

"Don't get your bowels in an uproar, Eddie. I'll just sit myself down and watch for a while. It wouldn't offend you if I giggled now and then? Okay, I'll just sit here and watch."

"Gentlemen, I return to the subject of the Low Stakes Gambling Act. It is obviously an unpopular measure, but we must remember that those of us who live within our means will all be able to afford a small sacrifice for the betterment of our community."

"I beg to differ with you on that point, Sir." Nobody had yet been able to pronounce the name of the new Middle School Principal the same way twice, so he had modestly suggested they just call him "Professor P", and it had stuck with him long enough to make everyone comfortable. "The salary I receive for the position I hold in this town is slightly less than two-thirds of what I would receive in Denver for an equivalent post, but it is enough that my family and I are comfortable ..."

"That's what you're being paid for, isn't it?"

"Absolutely not! I am paid to administer the finest education we can possibly offer to our children, and you have my solemn promise that is exactly what my life's goal is to be. Since the general public views the schools less as institutions of education and more as day-care centers they are never going to give us a salary any higher than the absolute minimum, but teachers realize they will be short-changed when they become teachers so there is no point in arguing about that. What I was trying to say is that our kids are going to be asking a whole lot of questions that I don't think you give them the credit to formulate, and I am not being paid a niggardly wage to support a clan of half-witted morons who seem to take some sort of maniacal pleasure out of public deception! I and my staff are personally responsible for the absolute future of your children and we evidently look upon this as a concept beyond your scope of imagination! Exactly what are the monies generated from this Gambling Act intended to fund, Mr. Chairman, renovation of the Town's sewer system? Your sewers are literally full of shit, Eddie, and your laws reflect a shining example of that policy."

'Professor P.' had been looked upon as a soft-spoken man who worked within the system. That was one of the major points that got him hired. This red-faced out-spoken guardian of the Middle School was not what had appeared on his resume, and that should have been enough to make any small time politico nervous. Eddie, it seemed, had missed the point.

"Professor, that Act was voted into law by the public and can only be taken off the roles by public vote. The earliest we could possibly schedule a vote would be in the May Primaries, and we would have a rough time getting the paperwork done by then. I think that realistically the earliest any of us could count on for a review of this matter would be by next November".

Anybody who's ever attended a Willie Nelson concert knows the chant to the song, but this wasn't a concert that Willie would attend.

"Bullshit!"

It came as an unison voice.

"That's uncalled for!"

"It's the Gambling that's uncalled for!" Ace was getting wound-up again. "And it wouldn't take until November to convict somebody of murder, so don't try to tell me there isn't time to drop a bad law. Nobody's going to challenge the legality of doing the right thing."

"Speaking of murder," came that earlier voice from the back of the room, "what do you hear from John Loughlin these days?"

"Just a minute! That was unnecessary." Maybe the Mayor's job wouldn't be so much fun after all. "If you know something about that terrible tragedy, the Police Station is on the first floor, but I will not have this meeting become a forum for rumors and gossip."

"It is not", said Ace, calmly standing and speaking in an almost-too-quiet voice, "rumor or gossip that a member of this community and of this board was violently murdered. It is also not something the Police Department or anybody else is releasing any information about. What it is, is it's something that's our Goddamned business to know," he continued, becoming more his old self again, "and the question the gentleman asked was, 'What do you hear from John Loughlin these days'."

"The Police will release that information as they see fit." Why were they being so persistent in asking him about it? He wasn't the one who had actually pulled the trigger, was he?

"Mr. Swanson," came that same Southern voice again, "I don't think it would be appropriate for any sensitive details concerning that case to be released and thereby jeopardizing the on-going investigation". Thank God, somebody in here's sane. "What is bothering us is that absolutely nothing about that on-going case has been released. Absolutely nothing. You must bump into the Chief of Police several times a day, so perhaps you could shed a little light on, if not the case itself, then why is it being made to look like there's a cover-up going on?"

"You don't even live here! What are you doing asking questions about our town?"

"Why are you avoiding answering them? Besides, this isn't an election being conducted here so the twenty five day residency stipulation doesn't apply. And it isn't just me asking questions, Sir!"

"You are out of control! You are all out of control! This meeting is adjourned!"

The coward's way out isn't always the worst way to go. The Council, save "Professor P" and "The New Woman", rose as one at the slam of the gavel and, with a less-than-graceful pirouette, split the room.

"Do you think he's hiding something?", she asked her colleague.

"Not very well." His answer seemed to reflect the thoughts of a lot of people around the town these days.

*   *   *   *   *

John Loughlin was a good example of somebody who was old enough to know better, but didn't. His family was one of the oldest in town, going back to the beginning of the Century, but that gave him no right to make light of the fact that not everybody else in town had earned as much money as his family. He had become "Uppity", a "White Nigger", and that, the rest of the "Informed Counsel" knew, was the worst kind. The "Informed Counsel", as they referred to themselves, was comprised of a few members of the regular Town Counsel who had the insight to use their wisdom and experience in seeing the correct direction the town must travel in order to benefit best those who deserved it most. John Loughlin had once been a member of that inner circle, but he had begun to wander a little to the wrong side of the Right Thinkers a few years ago when he balked at the continuance of a tax levy that had been guaranteed to end with that fiscal year. That tax levy had long since bought and paid for it's original project, and what had been coming in since then had become a valued asset to the men who had engineered a corner of the school bonds to take up the slack that the levy wouldn't need to do any more. Get it? Creative accounting. That particular tax levy will soon need to be discovered by the Council to have gone on too long, and through the graciousness of that same Council will be taken off the books as soon as possible. Maybe particular attention will need to be given to the wording of the announcement of it's demise.

There had been three of the seven members of the regular Town Counsel who were "Informed", but their enthusiasm had dropped in reverse proportion to their numbers. Since the death of John Loughlin the remaining member didn't want to speak with Eddie Swanson anywhere other than in public, and then only about public matters. He no longer stopped by the Swanson home once or twice a week to sip Glenfiddich and discuss the inner-most workings of the Town. He made excuses to not be in his office with him, alone. He was acting afraid. Afraid of Eddie Swanson. "Well," thought Eddie to himself after the last remaining member had just made yet another excuse for not joining him for lunch, "he had a right to be afraid of me and he knew it. He also knew that he had

90

better keep his mouth shut or John Loughlin's seat wouldn't be the only one vacant at the Council." Eddie Swanson knew how to get things done.

*   *   *   *   *

There were seven members of the Town Council, if you counted the Mayor, which nobody did unless there was a tie vote. The Mayor wasn't powerless in his capacity as Mayor, but his actual participation in the function of the Town Council consisted mainly of taking a shower after work, before the Counsel convened. He presided over the six actual members and brought them to order, but mostly he sat politely through their incredibly boring proceedings and fielded most of the very few questions asked by the even fewer people who attended the meetings. He was a good guy, an honest man, was tired of being Mayor, and was disgusted with the council. They had been dick-dancing with both themselves and the town for several years and nobody was liking it very much. He hadn't missed last night's meeting out of disgust, however.   He had missed it because it wasn't a regular meeting and nobody had told him it was being held, which was just as well because he is about the only person on the Council who likes Ace Palmer and undoubtedly would have sided with him as much as Parliamentary proceedings would have allowed.

"Bloody idiots," Frank Parker muttered to his shoes.

"You say something, Dear?" He couldn't get much passed Elaine, but in Forty-some years of marriage he hadn't often tried.

"Just paying compliments to the Counsel. I think it's time I had a heart-to-heart with them."

"Still considering that audit?"

"It'd serve them right if they all spent their next few birthdays having a party in Canyon City. You know, Elaine, those boys have been up to something for quite a long time. I've already told you that enough times you're due for being tired of hearing about it," he sighed. "But now, there's a difference. I can't put my finger on it, but some kind of subtle change came over them after John was killed."

91

"A change came over all of us, Frank. It was a terrible thing and he was a dear friend." A change had certainly come over John Loughlin, and not just that he was dead. It was earlier. Somehow he had "altered his arrogance", for lack of a better term. He had gone from obnoxiously self-satisfied to obnoxiously smug, a delicate difference to be sure, but a detectable difference when you get to know a person well enough. "I think you're taking this whole episode too much to heart. For fourteen years you've been treating this town as though it was your second child, and now that it needs to be spanked you're having second thoughts."

"Bless you, Elaine, for making what clouds me so completely to become so clear. If only I could gain your perception." Sometimes when they spoke to each other it was as though they were speaking with the clarity of a cloud in the wind. It was one of the pure satisfactions gained of a lasting love.

"You have always had the same perception as me, Dear. That's one of the things that has made me love you for so long." She'd only been a Grandmother for nineteen years but sometimes she could make it sound like it had been her job all her life.

"You know they're screwing this town like a fat dog, and for the sake of the town it has to stop before that fat dog starts barking loud enough to wake the neighbors." When you've been a General Contractor for a bunch of years, the Grandmother you married not only understands your euphemisms but is able to respond in kind:

"Then grab them by the 'short-and-curlys', Frank, and twist 'em till it hurts."

*   *   *   *   *

In Corporate America there is a slight deception being perpetrated, only in this circumstance, contrary to the popular misconceptions among the general public, this deception is not only legal but welcomed by everyone involved. It isn't meant to be a secret so much as an unspoken convenience, and a convenience to all it is, for without it the Goods and Services we have all come to enjoy in our daily lives would be considerably obstructed. Not that we still couldn't stop by the Country Super Market for a prime loaf of Wonder's White, but it might not have the fine texture and delicate bouquet reminiscent of all those PB&J's we have enjoyed since we first savored them as kids. It isn't like we'd never again be able to drop by Delmar's for a tall riser of Budweiser, but it may not be the Prime Brew; the Older Budweiser. Our lives just wouldn't be the same if it weren't for Mike Hansen. Mike's the guy you call when you need things, any of them, and need them on time. Mike's the guy who takes the phone call which puts the order in the machine that types the invoice that gets posted for the goods which are delivered on time, every time. Mike makes a good salary for being so efficient at his job, and that in itself is almost a crime because Mike requires no salary. He has no wife, no kids, no home, no life. Mike Hansen, in fact, doesn't exist. Mike Hansen, in fact, is a job description filled by whoever gets hired to fill it.

It was found some time ago that when a client calls a supplier, the client likes to talk with the same person each time. It gives a sense of security and familiarity, sort of like always going to the same Physician. The problem with an Order Clerk's job is that it will simply never pay enough to attract the right people for the job and then give them any incentive to stick around long enough to give the customer the sense of security necessary to place an order with an "old friend". What Industry has devised, much to the satisfaction of all involved, is Mike Hansen. Regardless of who's filling the chair at the moment, it's Mike. It's simply a more efficient way of getting things done, so when the Town Council of Estes Park suggested hiring "Mike Hansen" to handle some of the more redundant chores that crop up in the administration of a small town, it made a good deal of sense to everybody. The council even had the foresight to take Mike Hansen one step farther; Mike worked in every office of every department in town, thereby sharing not only his cost throughout what nobody really thinks of as a bureaucracy but also sharing the wealth of having him universally available. He's a real handy fellow to have around, and since almost all of the deals are made by FAX there's not the usual gender barrier experienced by needing to match the name with the presumed sex. This frees the position to be filled by whomever needs to be him, and, by a lucky twist of administrative fate, everybody wanted to be Mike Hansen. Because of his flexibility within the offices, whenever anyone played the role, that person got to be Mike all day in addition to their usual duties. Since Mike was one of the highest paid employees the town had ever hired, the fifteen minutes or so spent in the capacity of Mike earned the lucky person what could amount to an extra day-and-a-half in wages. Nobody knew who was going to be Mike for the day any more than nobody knew if anyone was going to be Mike that day at all. A call would come to the Planning Department, for example, and whoever answered the phone would be told by the unidentified voice on the other end that if she could find a specific thing at a specific price, she could be "Mike For A Day!" She tried real hard to do it, too, and it usually paid off for her. Not always, and the times it didn't the guy on the other end of the phone had generally placed the order already with instructions that no identical orders be accepted. The old "Bait-and-Switch" trick that car dealers are so fond of maneuvering, but this time driven in reverse gear. That meant that each of the twenty three "girls" would get the job at least twice a year each, and some of the senior employees got to play the game even more often. Lucky them, and lucky that they wouldn't mind a little "Christmas Bonus" when it was needed most. If one of the women in the office were about to have a baby, for example, it was looked upon by all the others as an act of generosity by The Council when she got to be Mike Hansen three times during her last week before maternity-leave. After all, they were one big family in that building, weren't they?

Mike Hansen was kept busy thirteen weeks out of the year. Five days a week times 4.2 weeks per month times three months per year meant one quarter of the time the office was open, Mike was active. For the other thirty-nine weeks out of the year Mike was in the back pocket of the Informed Council. Literally in their back pocket, for where else would he be kept and still be convenient? Just a little extra something for their efforts. $42,000 per year divided five ways meant that "The Girls" split $8,400 between them, and the Informed Council divided the remaining $33,600 amongst it's three members. Except now there were only two members, and one of them didn't even pick up his share this week. The money wouldn't go to waste, though. Eddie Swanson wasn't a wasteful man.

*   *   *   *   *

"I think it may confuse him, particularly in his brain."

"That's not much of an answer, Pauli." We had met at The Wheel at his request. He seemed upset by last night's Council meeting. Everybody seemed upset by last night's Council meeting.

"If I had to put my finger on the nose of the person I suspect most likely to be behind the troubles in this little town, it would rest upon one bulbous and oily." Much to the delight of nearly everyone, Eddie Swanson had been voted "Beak of the Week" for several months running. "The problem is that all the evidence we have is circumstantial. Thoreau has been credited with saying something like, 'Some circumstantial evidence is just too strong to ignore. Like a Trout in the milk, for example'. I've never figured out just what he meant by that but I've always liked the expression, and this town, Jimmy, has 'a Trout in it's milk'."

"Look, our Cop Shop may have it's share of buffoons, but they're not all stupid and they're not all crooks. Don't you think they've been able to see what you see and do something about it?"

"Not necessarily, or, at least, not yet. Analogize it to the parents of a rapist who say their boy is 'simply excitable'. Complete denial on their part to what is so obvious to everyone else. Even if their boy is found guilty and he willingly admits his crime, they may never accept it. I called your police chief a ''gameshow host' once, and now I think that may be too kind, but other than maybe filling his wife's car from the Town's gas pump I seriously doubt he's much of a criminal. I don't think he's clever enough to be much of a criminal."

"Couldn't somebody just tell him?"

"Tell him what?"

"Tell him what's going on behind his back. Tell him there's more than somewhat of a bit of corruption here."

"Probably not. He wouldn't listen. He's 'in denial' and couldn't imagine such a thing happening in his town. Even if he did see it, I doubt he would confront Swanson because he's also a coward."

"Coward?"

"Coward. And a bully. There's no other reason for him to have hired the idiots that staff his Department if he didn't need

95

somebody who'd jump when he barked and kowtow when he passed by."

"Not all of the cops are idiots."

"I thought you didn't like them."

"I don't like the way they conduct themselves, but I don't know them personally. Sort of like the difference between a town and a community. Anyway, it doesn't need to be the Chief who blows the whistle on them. Or even a cop, for that matter. What if I were to send a well-written letter to the Governor requesting the C.B.I. look into it?"

"Is that what you want to do?"

"Of course not, but only because I enjoy keeping a low profile. It's purely a hypothetical question, but wouldn't that work?"

"Not yet, no, because without a strong suspicion that The Chief is directly involved, he'd be the first one they'd contact. If nothing else, that would alert whoever is behind any wrong doings to back-off, and there goes the case. From this point the best we can hope for is for something really solid to happen."

"What would be solid enough to make you happy?"

"Something Federal like a car bomb or a bank robbery would be nice. Kidnapping. Not another murder because that's not Federal, and if it were all to go away today I doubt it would ever get solved."

"You're really getting into this, aren't you?"

"Nope. In fact, I'm getting out of it. Heading back to The City in the morning. Have fun."

Chapter Eight

The greatest limitation to the amount of revenue to be generated in Estes Park is parking, and every available inch of ground has long been taken. Hell, only three of the eleven existing parking lots in the "Greater Metro Estes Area" are on level ground, and one of those is a dinky little twenty three-unit lot put in when the local A&W closed. Maybe 4.2 million people a year didn't like the best Root Beer in the world well enough to support one stupid Drive-In. Maybe they did and there was a different reason A&W couldn't make a go of it, but what happened was that the A&W got torn down, Ace Palmer bought the I-Beams that made-up and held-up the canopy, then four inches of asphalt got laid over about the same amount of aggregate and twenty three more cars could be parked in town even if it was in the outer reaches of where somebody might want to walk to buy a rubber tomahawk, given their druthers for the route downtown. High-rise structures had often been proposed, but nobody wanted to block the view, even if the view consisted of nothing other than The Bank. That was a phobia shared by all the town's merchants even though most of them were in Texas or Arizona more than half of the year and couldn't see the mountains regardless of what the view might be. The town has gone through quite a face lift during the last ten years, and while it was perhaps considered to be more esthetically pleasant to have quaint little shops and a fountain that runs five months a year where there was once a clapboard grocery store and a small parking lot that was open all year, many of the town's visitors had openly worried that "their little town" might become too modern. It was becoming too modern in some respects in that, sort of like when the cops would turn their backs on a Missouri license plate making an illegal U-Turn but would bust a local for breathing through the wrong nostril, if the word got out that any of the view was being obstructed there was the dominant fear that people would not come. Or, at least, not stop on their way through.

One attempt to relieve some of the pressure on downtown parking was implemented by asking locals working downtown to park in the outlying areas and take the Trolly-bus into town, thus freeing about a hundred parking places. This plan, like so much of what the Town Council designed for locals, was flawed from it's inception. By having the Trolley begin it's daily rounds an hour after most of the shops opened and stop running two hours before they closed, it was impossible for it to be used by those for whom it was supposedly intended, and the scheme was doomed before it began. It also didn't take into consideration the cynical view most minimum-wage earners hold toward their wealthy employers. As often as not, when an employee was chided by the employer for using a municipal lot and thereby "not being part of the team", the employee had parked next to the boss's car. Some shop owners had attempted to get the offending autos ticketed and towed, which worked great until about fifteen minutes into the execution of the plan when the owner of a particularly successful tomahawk shop spotted his own car going down Main Street backwards, ass-in-the-air behind a tow truck, whence the popularity of the entire program took a sudden but not unexpected nose-dive.

So the high-rise parking idea may have to wait until there are so many people crawling around the Town the scenery is blocked-out anyway. Parking in non-congested out-lying areas won't work until the Trolly schedule is taken even semi-seriously, such as being planned by someone more intelligent than a demented four-year-old. And it will need to be paid for at least in part by the Merchants who will reap the benefits of the open parking places because you know that the Town Fathers aren't going to cough-up a nickel more than they need to, if that.

The only other parking alternative would be sub-terrainian parking, but there's a basic flaw in that one, too; drainage, with a capital Drain. With rivers running on each side of a three-hundred-yard-wide valley that's lined with rock, if the Summer rains or Winter snows didn't flood an underground structure Mother Nature's seepage would do it because, short of half mile of pipe to the lake (which would carry not only the water to the closest feasible site but also all of the motor oil and tire rubber inherent in such a structure) there's nowhere else for it to go. In fact, the only thing that ran

98

underground in town other than a few power lines was the labyrinth of sewer lines built randomly over an eighty year period.

Those sewer lines had been a nuisance to build from their inception through the rock and rocky soil to a depth where they wouldn't freeze in Winter, and originally they had not gone much farther than the edge of the builder's property before a convenient stream was found into which they could be dumped. With the increase in population came the necessity to end this practice. This was done by consolidating the sewer systems into fewer and fewer lines until they could all eventually come together into some sort of terminal which would then feed a treatment plant. Before they congregated as the one it was necessary to congregate the many into several, and then those several into few, and eventually they would all congregate into the common commode where the effluent would be stirred and aerated and made fit to feed to the fish. So it was decided by those who were voted-in to make such decisions that it would be most efficient (read: Cheapest) to create a whole bunch of little vertical culverts scattered around the town where three or four little lines would make one larger line. This line would then converge with it's counterparts, and so on until a couple of fifteen-inchers found their way down that last quarter mile stretch from the lower downtown area into the Treatment Plant itself. Like the upside-down root system of a tree. The last vertical culvert from the Northern Sector sat at the East end of the Municipal parking lot which served the Library, The Municipal Building, and The Estes Savings Bank (the ownership of which was now in severe litigation by the heirs of John Loughlin). This was a magnificent culvert; at four feet in diameter with foot-holds molded into the concrete to augment the steel hand-rails bolted to the wall, this was no paltry "pipe". Under the massive steel hat it wore at street-level and located seven-and-a-half-feet below the pavement was a grating where a man could stand straight up in Winter and do the maintenance he came to do, and do it with the comfort of dry feet. With it's own lighting system and a phone jack that connected directly to Sewer Central, the natural warmth of this culvert would have made it an outstanding example of the possibilities of low-cost vertical housing had it not been for the smell of what kept it naturally warm. The four-inch pipe in the North side draining The Bank was

99

insignificant compared to the eight-inch line which served the South side of the block, but both put together paled in the shadow of the magnificent ten-inch wonder which entered the culvert from the West, directly between the other two. The sole purpose of this ten-inch beauty, it's raison d'etre, was to care for the services of the Library and the Municipal Building. A total of eleven toilets, five urinals, three sinks, and a small shower stall in the Fire Station. A garden hose would have almost done as well if you could get the turds to slide through, but a ten-inch pipe is what the architect of the buildings wanted and a ten-incher is what he got. It was in fact so large, it was observed, that a medium sized Raccoon could easily crawl up it and die, and to this end steel bars were welded into the mouth of the pipe at it's culvert end. The "jailhouse" effect did nothing to detract from the overall appearance of the interior of The Culvert however; the sinister nature of it enhanced it's general mystique. This was a Showcase Culvert if ever one had been built and it is a darn shame that more people can't appreciate quality in sewer culverts they way they appreciate quality in the cars they drive above them, even though it's been said that if people knew quality in cars they'd ride bicycles. But people don't know cars and they don't know culverts, and this one would have lived it's useful life in total anonymity had Tony Engleman not found it, had not taken this culvert as his own to Champion the Cause of "Freedom for his People". Maybe Tony Engleman could have lived his useful life if his pursuit of this culvert hadn't caused him to die.

*　　*　　*　　*　　*

Nothing like having somebody come up behind you when you're deep in thought and expect to be alone. "One of these times you're going to get both of us in a lot of trouble. What are you doing off the reservation this time of night, trying to become an honest man?"

"Cruising". It wasn't night and Tony Engleman was neither cruising nor, I suspected, being honest. I've watched this guy "cruise" and he could make some incredible time, but just that he had stopped long enough to talk meant that either he wasn't cruising or he's already done it. "Going to fly that thing after all?"

He was making reference to my motor-glider, a radio-controlled model aircraft that spun the propeller with an electric motor of about the same power as those .049 gas engines we played with as kids. The electric motor gave me the ability to use the radio to turn it off to let the plane glide, then restart it when it got too close to the ground. At sea level, three five-hundred-foot climbs could be expected, but at this elevation I didn't have the foggiest idea what it would do. Building model airplanes has long been a hobby of mine, albeit a passive hobby, and this was the first one I had completed in about two years. Fiddling with all those little sticks forces me to relax in order to not break them, so the end product of the actual building wasn't always to put them in the air. Sometimes I just built a plane for the pleasure of building a plane. This one had began life as a "flyer", though, and it was time to put it in the air. The nervousness I was feeling wasn't so much about the loss of a couple hundred dollars of equipment because it was designed as a slow flyer and in the event of the worst crash I could still expect the radio gear to come out alive. I was simply nervous in general which was a justified emotion because I'm an inexperienced glider-guider and figured I had a fifty-fifty chance of not re-kitting the plane on touchdown. Take-offs are optional; landings are mandatory. I'd say I'm stalling the launch, but "stall" is a nasty word around aircraft. Two-point-six pounds of assorted wood and electronics assembled at my leisure over a six month period. The control surfaces worked correctly, the battery was charged, the motor was armed, and the radio was turned on. No reason not to find out how much I enjoy this hobby after all. Lots of fun. This was the first flight.

"With any luck I have it balanced right and the air will be cool enough to give me enough density to get it up."

"How much density do you need to get it up?" It isn't so much what Tony says as how he says it that gets the message through. All the subtlety of a 36-D Cup that's been stuffed with Kleenex to make it look good.

"At this elevation, thirty degrees of temperature the air is not quite as dense as it would be at a hundred degrees at sea level, so consider us today being somewhere in the Sahara Desert without the benefit of a nice tan, but if it got any colder it won't be fun. Want to watch? You could think of it as an Eagle, your namesake." I enjoyed baiting Tony because I could never be sure what he could come up with when he got moved emotionally.

"Thanks, but I've got to take off. So do you. That's a pun." Wherever it was he was going, it wasn't here with me. The only thing on this end of the lake other than a small community park were the Public Schools, all nestled together where they could be watched as one. "I'm supposed to meet some guys here to shoot some hoops in the Gym. Want to shoot a hoop after you splash your plane?"

"If this thing crashes I might be in the mood for it, yes. Got any specific 'Hoop' in mind?"

"Bite me", he grinned.

I should accept the offer. I know Tony doesn't "shoot hoops" because he says the expression brings bad Karma to Indians. No telling what he's up to. "No, I'm going to try for a few flights and go home. Want to come over for dinner?"

"I'm having dinner with Rev. Simms, but thanks anyway. Might catch a ride back to town with you if you don't mind."

"I'll watch for you when I leave." And he was gone. I swear he knows how to evaporate at will.

The flight, by the way, was uneventful other than for the few times my heart stopped. When Hobby Lobby says they've got a good beginner's plane they aren't blowing smoke. I set it up the way they said I should and any problems the "Skimmer" had were pilot-induced. I got about five minutes of motor time from each of the two sets of 1200 MAH Nicad battery packs I brought, which added up to about ten minutes per flight including gliding time with the motor off. I'll be more relaxed next time I come out, I hope, and should be able to stretch that to half-again as much air time. By the time I'd broken the plane into bite-sized pieces, meaning removing the wing from the fuselage so I could fit it into "PIGRON", the trunk was being opened and something was being tossed in. "Be sure to get it shut with the handle pointing straight down, Tony." I didn't have to look to see who it was, and I didn't want to look to see what he'd stashed in my car.

"How'd it go?" Nice of him to ask because he probably did care, but I don't think he was interested in an answer.

"It flew twice, and will fly at least once more if I can get it home without inflicting too much 'hanger rash'. Where you off to?"

102

"The 'Reservation' would be good about now," he giggled. The little bastard was up to something.

"You score what you came after?" By asking it like that, he wouldn't feel obliged to lie about what he'd done.

"Consider it a recreational endowment. A donation from The Parks Department to The Good Guys. They're definitely going to want to 'shoot a hoop' for this one." At that he just shut the door of the car and slumped into the seat, slobbering in comical hysteria.

He wasn't going to be any use to anyone, not for a few minutes. Time to escape from the scene of the crime.

"You got any outstanding warrants?"

"Probably. I don't know. Which way's the wind blowing? Why do you ask?"

"I don't ask, but Buford's coming up behind us fast and I don't want to have to explain to that P.D.C.B. all about what it is that I don't know what you put it my trunk."

"P.D.C.B.?"

"Poor Dumb Clueless Bastard." I generally reserve those initials for tourists, but Buford qualifies for a category all his own. "You're in my car, and if you have a warrant that gives him the right to search my car."

"I'm clean, and I have the paperwork to prove it." Tony is one of those guys who gets busted so often for such not-shit complaints that he finds it easier to just carry an official transcript of his last court preceding than to try to get anyone to take his word for something. The local cops don't like him and he knows it, so he covers-his-ass as best he can. Thanks, Tony. I appreciate it. "Isn't that the same cop that hassled you when you brought us those groceries?", he asked, looking back through the tiny little rear window.

"Yep. I call him 'Buford'. You know him?"

"Not in the Biblical sense, but I've seen him around a lot lately. I understand he has a serious head injury".

"Such as?"

"He has a small amount of brain tissue lodged in his skull. And he eats Coma-Toasties for breakfast." I think Tony was on a roll. "Look, I'm going to find a quick way onto the Reservation when you pull over, so the closer you get me to the fence, the more I'll like it."

"You just said you're clean".

"I am, but that doesn't mean I plan on staying that way".

"Why not? Do you enjoy getting hassled?"

Grinning like a 'possum eating shit, that twinkle in his eyes answered my question. "Okay, when I pull over I'm going to slide into the ditch and knock a hole in the oil pan. Help me take a look at it, and that will get us both out of the car and walking around. Just don't give him a reason to shoot you or he might start thinking I'm on your side and go into a self-defence mode with me, too."

The fact is that the Cops have the Badges and the Guns and the Courts and any interpretation of the law they want to have, and as nice as it is to sit out of ear-shot and bad-mouth the legal system, they scare me shitless. They can do anything they want and unless F. Lee Bailey is in your corner you can be hung out to dry at their slightest whim. The positive side of the coin is that if I am exceptionally correct in what I'm doing I have a better than fifty-fifty chance of eventually going free during my natural life. Nobody likes the ridiculous law-suit judgments being offered by the courts these days, nobody other than the few plaintiffs who win and the many attorneys who represent them, but those judgments seem to have set the precedence for the outcome of many judicial proceedings. We're all running scared when it comes to legal matters.

The ground clearance on 'PIGIRON' is almost as good as that of an old VW Van, and with the wheels as close together as they are it can go into a pretty deep ditch before anything hanging under the car touches anything protruding from below. If you haven't crawled under it, however, and are used to driving the "Modern" cars like those developed since the late Fifties, you'd expect it to scrape something while going into a ditch. The fact is, I was only pulling into what amounted to not much more than a shallow rut so far as the car was concerned, but that could be a little secret between 'PIGIRON' and myself.

"God damn it!", I hollered as I whipped out of the car and dropped to the ground to inspect the "damage".

"Hey, Jimmy, thanks for the ride", Tony offered from his position under the frame on the other side.

"Good luck, Buddy".

"Piece of cake".

I brushed-off the dirt I'd gotten on my knees with the dirt I'd gotten on my hands and jumped back in the driver's seat. "What would be the problem, Officer?" It was back to the old "let's be straight with each other" tom-foolery, and my tone of voice indicated that my mood was justifiably unpleasant.

"I want to talk with him," jutting his chin at my passenger in a way that would make Kirk Douglas proud. I guess he hadn't noticed that Tony had opened and then closed the door without ever getting in.

"So talk to him. Do I need to be detained, too?"

"What's that thing in the back seat?" Felony 'Hobby Lobby Skimmer' possession. What a way to do hard time!

"If it's what you stopped me for, I'll be leaving now." I'm scared, but he's stupid, which should make all of us even more scared. It's The Law, and it's scary.

"Don't get smart with me."

"Okay, I'll be stupid with you, but please speak into the envelope." It was the only time in my life I could remember being glad for getting "Junk Mail"; I had picked up a small manila envelope from some society which wanted yet another pre-pubescent girl to grow old enough to make me think she could ever become a mail-order bride who would possibly accept my minor weenie to the point that they were actually sending audio tapes through the mail in order to get a donation. "Manila" envelopes is an especially appropriate name for them in this case. I collect the little stick-ums they give me, but I don't send them any money because somewhere in the back of my mind I amuse myself with the idea that this will make them stop clogging my PO Box with their crap. This package, however, was large enough to have held a tape recorder if you were so blatantly stupid to even think that it might. If that was the case, you deserved whatever you got.

"I ain't speaking into anything."

"You're speaking into my window, but for the sake of argument let's say that you aren't speaking and neither am I. I'm on my way now, if you don't mind."

"You think you're pretty clever, don't you?" Cops get to ask all the best questions.

"No, I don't think that of anyone here." He didn't get it, but I'd better back-off before he called in somebody who might. People like this frighten me.

In the meantime, Tony had quietly opened the trunk, removed his goodies, and was off and over the fence of the Oliver Property before either of us saw him. Once Buford realized what was going on he got a look on his face like a kid with his hand in the cookie jar.

"Come back here, boy, I want to talk to you and I'm not finished yet", he shouted after Tony. Poor 'Buford'. I'm going to have to learn his name, yet. He tries so hard to be good it ought to make his Mamma proud. Tony, by this time, was clearly on Federal Property and out of his jurisdiction, and Buford knew that, no matter how little he was letting on.

"You ain't never been in 'direct pursuit'," Tony hollered, "so blow me!"

"You want to see my license and registration, Officer?" Least I could do at this point was be friendly to Buford. Somebody had to and it wasn't going to be Tony. In all the years I've been driving I have deserved many tickets and the fact is that I have never gotten one. This douche-bag was starting to get to me to the point that I didn't really care if my lucky streak ran out now or not but there's no point in pushing it, so I smiled at him, then he smiled at me, and I just drove off, and he just let me.

Hadn't he radioed anybody to tell them he had stopped me and let them know what he was doing? Maybe this wasn't so scary after all. Maybe it is scary and I don't know it.

*   *   *   *   *

Valleys are formed by an abundant something finding a soft spot between two mountains and moving stuff with it on the way down. Glaciers do a nice and highly visual job of it, but most often it's the wind and water that do the moving. In the case of Estes Park, four different rivers had converged from three directions into an ancient hollow with a high, narrow outlet to deposit their

106

alluvium. Over the millennia these deposits had filled that hollow to form a crescent-shaped flat space, the two-square-mile park from which the town took it's name. Deer and Elk came to live side by side there, a near perfect Winter feeding ground with acres of tender native grasses surrounded by a dense protective forest. Coyotes and wolves came for the squirrels and rabbits and woodchucks which flourished during the months the little guys could be above ground and not hibernating, and the Black Bear just sort of hung around. Add the Eagles and Owls and Ravens that stuck through the Winter and you have a scene that would bring tears to Walt Disney's eyes if not his bank account. No wonder so many varied types of people come up here; all sorts of "animals" like the area. The Indians walked through the Valley during the Summer and built some strange rock walls and wooden totems in the hills around it, but for their own reasons they never chose to live here year-round. The first individual humans who did settle the area on a permanent basis used cattle as an excuse, but the cattle didn't flourish any better than the Elk with which they were competing for food. Bad idea, bringing cattle into the valley, but fortunately they went away for the most part after only a few years, although some of the ranchers stayed on to do other things. When the hoiti-toiti started arriving in the latter 1800's they brought with them an embryonic version of what we have today; working-class people serving the land-holding class serving the rich, or at least anyone sporting a bankroll they were willing to leave behind. Not to knock the rich guys. How they got their money is their business, and to criticize them simply for having it is right up there with racial prejudice; it sucks. They came here a hundred years ago for the same reason we still come here today and if we belittle them for that, well, there's always the Trickle-Down Theory to consider. The rich folks are just fine. They represent the best and the worst, just like the blue-collars, but they carry a higher profile so are a public target of ridicule the rest of us get to avoid. Prejudice. But up until The War the main influx of "non-locals" were the wealthy and their hangers-on of artists and actors and the toadies who trailed behind them. Same pecking order as today, the big difference between then and now is clothing styles and sheer numbers of tourists who can be accommodated. Back then, though, the roads were lousy and the trek was arduous. After The War, things changed.

The Department of Reclamation built a concrete dam across the outlet from the valley during the Depression Years, back when building dams seemed like a good idea, and a large shallow lake formed over the historic alluvium to become a back-up water source for the people living in the valley below. As the popularity of the area increased during the Post-War years and the roads into the valley improved, swimming and boating and fishing in the lake became it's own drawing card and soon a set of rules for conduct in and around the lake were written to ensure that everyone would be able to enjoy the water while still protecting it to keep it safe to drink. Not that anybody who lived here actually drank the water from the lake, but it seemed like an generous gesture on the part of the people who originally made the rules. At least, in retrospect, once social awareness became such that quietly bragging about it might have a positive effect on tourism it became understood that this had always been the idea.

Fishing was banned on the first two hundred yards of the lake at the West end because that's where three of the rivers, now converged, entered. Since trout are known to swim upstream when they feed it was openly agreed that it would be unsportsmanlike to take them from such a natural fish trap, and with the State Hatchery releasing millions of trout annually less than four miles upstream there were always a bunch of fish assembled in that first two hundred yards. The Town Fathers nodded at this with agreement and smiled in understanding while they hoped-to-shit that nobody ever tested the quality of the water where the river met the lake because otherwise there might be embarrassing questions asked about the standards of the Water Treatment Plant located there. Not that the plant didn't do an excellent job treating the 375,000 gallons of water that passed through in a slow day, but there are some things a treatment plant can't remove and nobody on the Town Council wanted to explain how they got there. Besides, it wasn't that anybody who lived here actually drank that water.

One thing that nobody ever got around to openly banning at the Lake was the use of outboard motors. Nobody even put a limit on the size of the motors used but, due to the relatively small area of the lake, anything over about five horsepower was a waste of time. In fact, the only people who ever abused it was a group of locals who had gotten together on the first day of Spring every year for the last Thirty years to go water-skiing, and that was tolerated in the name of tradition. Put two dozen small sailboats tacking in the Summer breeze with half that many motor boats each trolling for "the big one", and the lake was comfortably full. If you added the little paddle-boats the kids scuttled around the shore there were places where the Lake seemed almost congested, but it was good clean family fun and a welcome respite from the bustling streets less than a mile away.

As an act of good faith, the Marina kept it's outboard motor fuel well away from the Lake. In a cluster of five three-hundred gallon tanks hooked together in series so that they could be filled at the beginning of the summer and, theoretically anyway, be emptied one at a time until by the time the boats were hauled-out at the end of the season, there would be only one single tank with any gas left in it at all. With the unseasonably warm weather this fall the "season" ran on for nearly a month longer than it had in any of the last ten years and the fuel supply became dangerously low enough that the executive decision was made to fill the tanks. With the difference in the price per gallon between the one hundred gallons that would probably carry the Marina to the point where the lake would freeze and the thirteen hundred gallons the tanks would hold to be "topped-off", the Marina chose to "fill 'em up" and be ready for next Spring. After all, gasoline doesn't freeze and it won't rot so let's make the investment this year and take the cost-of-doing-business tax write-off while we can. It isn't exactly legal to store gasoline above ground, but the precautions taken had satisfied the EPA for the time-being, especially with the promise from The Town Council that more than enough would be done next year to satisfy everyone well into the next decade. That five tanks would be full rather than one tank would be holding "just some" wasn't anything that the EPA would be bothered with; those guys are too busy as it is. The way things turned-out not nearly as much gas had been used before the lake finally froze as was anticipated, but the Marina was ready for the next year. And this was good.

Chapter Nine

I could never tell when to expect Tony Engleman to show up at my house. I could never tell when Tony Engleman would show up anywhere, but I was at home when he showed up this time, and I wasn't expecting it. He'll come any time of day, knowing I'll have a cool Bud in the refrigerator and he's always welcome to it. He rarely asks for one right away, but if the offer isn't made he usually gets around to it before too long, and that's fine by me. I actually said "no" today, just to see how he'd react, and he took it like a real trooper. He grinned that stupid grin of his and pulled a Bud out of his jacket, then he pulled out another and handed it to me, and then he stepped out to the front porch and brought in the rest of the half-rack he'd stashed before he knocked on the door. Tony brings almost as much beer as he drinks, and if he didn't ever bring any I wouldn't care, although I'd try to never let onto it. About the only thing I will seriously deny him is a taste of Jim Beam. Tony can drink beer all day, but give him a shot of whisky and that old scum about Indians not being able to hold their liquor floats right to the surface. But he wasn't drinking Beam today. He was hardly even drinking the Bud he was warming between his hands. He was just sitting there, grinning like a 'Possum eating shit, and looking at me with his eyes on fire.

"You aren't required to say anything, Tony. Just you being here, sharing this space, sitting in my chair, smelling the way you smell, why, that's enough to carry anyone through the early afternoon."

Nothing. Just Tony and his grin and that awful smell. What had that 'Possum been doing before lunch, rolling in it?

"Ready for another?" He hadn't had any more of his first one in the fifteen minutes he'd been sitting there than he'd had any conversation, and I wanted to get him going sometime today.

"I got them, Jimmy, and they don't even know it yet. With luck, they won't have a clue for hours. The longer, the better." With that, he inhaled the beer in one swallow, crushed the can into a little aluminium spitwad, and got up for another. I had put his remaining ten-pack in the refrigerator, and it was like The Marx Brothers watching him try to fetch one. He got up, walked to the refrigerator, opened the door, grabbed a beer, then closed the door. Then he opened the door, put the beer back in, and returned to his chair. Got back up, went back to the 'frige, and closed the door, then opened the door and took a beer and set it in the sink, closed the door, and sat back down. Got up, went over, opened the door, took the beer out of the sink, closed the door, returned, and sat. Up, back, over, open, out, close, sit. Two beers, both of which were balanced in his left hand and neither of which was open. About the time he stood for his third Budweiser I intervened on behalf of both of us and took one from him.

"What's up, Buckwheat?"

"Buford. He pissed me off."

"I think he has that effect on most people and gets a regular paycheck for doing it. It's his job. He's a cop, and you don't like cops, so he pisses you off."

"Yeah, but Buford's special. He has a certain way of getting to me, so I made a special way of getting to him. I already did it, and he don't know it."

"Did what?"

"I thought you'd never ask. He came up to the 'Reservation' the night before last and told us we had to leave. He said that he and everyone else in town was tired of being embarrassed by our illegal actions, and he was going to do something about it. You remember John Chism, the Indian Lawyer? He asked Buford, and asked him very nicely, to no longer bother us. Buford told John to blow him because he was the 'new law' in this town. John said something like it was Buford who was doing the trespassing and suggested that if a few less over-weight, middle-class, pig-faced, gun-toting, red-neck, ass-breath, rotten-toothed ..., and that's when Buford just turned and kicked Po' square in the chops." Then Tony got frighteningly still. The comedy of the beers was gone and his mood-swing was almost distracting. He became as serious as I have ever seen anybody become, and his speech became clipped as he stared at the floor and began to relate his tale. "Po' wasn't doing anything other than being Po' and wanting to chase a 'something', and he kicked her. She

111

started choking because she had a Po' rock in her mouth and when he kicked her I guess she half-swallowed it. She was acting like she wanted to fall down but she couldn't, and that's the first time I ever saw her try to bite anybody. She got this high-pitched squeal coming from deep down inside her belly, real weird like she'd been eating grass and was trying to cough it up, and I think she went for him. I couldn't really tell 'cause when she leapt at him her soul was there but so was Buford's gun and Po' and the gun went off at the same time. She fell short of the mark by too many feet to have been a threat, but, God damn it, she went for him. Something in her past, something in her breeding came out. Something from somewhere down the line of her evolution suddenly and unexpectedly rose to the occasion, but it took that little pause that the last few hundred years of breeding took to develop what everyone likes about her. Liked about her. She went down good, man, and I never sold her to anyone."

"You mean, when I dropped you off yesterday, Po' was dead?"

"Yup."

"You didn't tell me."

"I know. I was there too, remember? I didn't tell anybody. I was afraid you'd want to do something to help, or maybe keep an eye on me. You know how friends can get in the way."

Yeah I did. Don't we all.

"I wanted to do something for Po'. I wanted to do something to the entire fucking town, but what can one crazy Indian do, short of murder? Something for them to remember Po' by, something in her name."

The twinkle returning to his eyes told me that he'd resurrected Po', at least in his own mind.

"You know that high sewer by the library?"

I knew which one he meant. It was just inside the lower Eastern end of the Library parking lot, and as magnificent as that culvert may have been under the ground, it was a pain in the ass above ground. Whether because the people who laid the sewers weren't the people who laid the parking lot weren't the people who laid the guy signing the check for the job once it got done isn't relevant. It wasn't right to have the top of it an inch-and-a-half above the surface of the pavement, but it wasn't so far off as to be worth fixing. A little circular ramp of asphalt ringing it's parameter kept tires from being knocked off the cars that bumped against it and everyone driving through that end of the lot soon learned to avoid it. Or they didn't.

"After Po' died, Buford went over to talk to Reverend Simms. I don't know what The Rev' told him, but Buford stomped away mad. I grabbed a pry-bar and headed for the Muni looking to break something, but before I got to any of the buildings I saw the manhole cover. It had always gotten on my nerves and seemed to be the physical manifestation of what I think of our Town Government so I got to figuring that if I just popped the top off, it wouldn't take very many cars getting a tire dumped into that sucker to create a lot of heat for the man with the fuzzy balls."

Creative thought is just that; Creative. Tony's train of thought began to wander then and I wanted to hear the rest of the story, so I gave him a little nudge.

"And?"

"And I lifted the lid to that culvert with the pry bar, and then I got this hell-of-an-idea. So I put the lid back in place and went back home, back to the 'Reservation', to work it out. I worked it out."

This time when he went to get another beer it was as a man with a purpose.

"When you were flying your airplane I was snagging basketballs from the school. Every basketball I could find, and a hand pump and a needle to fill them."

"Weren't they already full?"

"Yup, but they needed to be emptied first before they could be used. Then they needed to be filled again."

"Why?", I asked.

"Because otherwise they wouldn't fit between the bars."

"And which bars might these be, The Wheel and Mike's Place?"

"The ones in the sewer."

*   *   *   *   *

113

It is common knowledge among those who build dwellings that the cheapest per-square-foot method of construction is a basement. At about one third the cost of above-ground fabrication, it is the method of favor to put the maximum number of square feet within a prescribed tract of land. To this end, when the "Muni" was originally built, the goal was to stuff as many offices within the confines of these boundaries as is physically possible and do it at the lowest cost. Both the State and the County had been enlisted to chuck-in funds for the development of the building, so room needed to be made for the offices they felt were rightfully theirs. Because it was no more feasible to dig a basement in the Municipal Building than to build underground parking, a forty-foot long by fifteen-foot wide "well" was dug about three feet deep in the foyer to reduce the height necessary for the bloody thing to have enough head-room to make "Code", at least in a small but significant portion of the building. The Lord knows that the Town Fathers were primarily interested in satisfying "Code". By digging that "well", one third less material was needed for the walls around it, and while it wasn't a significant percentage of the price of the building, it was still a sizable chunk of change. When the second floor was completed, it's roof line just matched that of the over-sized height of the Fire Department wing at the north end. A smooth transition in architecture, and having the price lowered simply by digging a shallow hole was a brilliant idea. It also offered a few subliminal assets that weren't figured into the original equation but turned out to be just fine. When a person approached the desk where the water and electric and gas bills were paid, he did so from below. The "payee" was on a lower tier, and God help anybody trying to request an extension of his payment from that level. The person with whom he was speaking was already looking down at him, and that advantage carries many psychological leverage points in any situation regardless of who is doing the talking. Considering the attitude of the people who worked in the Muni it was a wonder that anyone would want to speak to them at all, but sometimes there was simply no alternative. This was a fearful lot, and for all the fear they tried to evoke they harbored just as much. They were afraid of their bosses, afraid of the public, and afraid for their jobs. Contained within the walls of the Municipal Building were sixty one percent of

114

all the jobs in town that offered a steady weekly paycheck, a retirement program, health insurance, job security, and a regular vacation. Real jobs. They were so real that they almost took the fun out of living in Estes Park, almost removed the challenge of getting-by in a very seasonal environment. Like wanting to have a mountain retreat and then constructing a tract house, these jobs have no personality. But neither do the people holding the jobs. They don't need a personality. What the peolpe holding the jobs needed was to show up for work every day for twenty years and then move to Apache Junction for the rest of what they thought passed for a life, and their manner of dealing with the public reflected that train of thought. They were the fourth "feifdom"; a ruling class all to themselves. They had the power to shield their bosses from harm and receive blessings for doing so. They had the power to record or not record a utility payment on time, to direct or not direct people to the Building Inspector, to garble an important message. Within their ranks was the strictest of hierarchies, but none of the employees of the many bureaucracies housed within the Municipal building was without power or influence or dignity. Until the toilets backed up.

It started slowly at first, of course. One of the stools in the Ladies room simply refused at accept any more effluent about half-way through an otherwise successful flush, and a gallon of water and most of what it was carrying went over the brim and onto the floor. That caused embarrassment for the woman doing the flushing because she knew what the first question to be asked was going to be, and she didn't think it was anybody's bitchiness that she'd gone through menopause two years earlier. Then the toilet vomited again in a satirical reversal of a teenage party on Saturday night, and then it did it again. Nothing the "old girl" could do now except flee in panic, secure only in the knowledge that she hadn't done either of those last two flushes. Or the third, which she failed to notice because by this time she was already out the door and seeking the sanctity of her desk.

Her little secret wasn't much of a secret for very long. Not only did the water out of that toilet ignore the drain that had been installed in the floor just for such an event, but both the drain and the other commode had joined in the chase, and that chase had, by this time, found it's way under the door. That particular door was located on a little platform halfway between the rear entrance to the building and the first step down to the well, and the two of them would have probably split the load between them had it not been for the air-tight seals recently installed under the doors in the name of Energy Conservation. In the name of Energy Conservation, every flush of every toilet in the Muni, Fire Station, and Library was being deposited in the "well" of the Foyer, and from there, there was no where else for it to go.

In the time it took for the first maintenance man to get to the scene of the crime, the entire floor of the foyer was being soaked by an ever increasing cascade of water. Eleven toilets, five urinals, three sinks, and a small shower may not be much for a ten-inch sewer pipe, but they can make quite the contribution to a forty-by-fifteen, six hundred square foot foyer. Three feet deep. One thousand eight hundred cubic feet of Municipal septic tank, and it was filling fast.

The second maintenance man came equipped with toilet plungers, which were the first line of defense brought to the war. Those did nothing more than discharge sewer water that would otherwise have gone straight to the floor first onto the walls and the toilet paper hanging on those walls and especially the clothing of the people manipulating the plungers before it went straight to the floor.

It was the third person to arrive on the scene who had the clearest head of the lot, and he wasn't even a maintenance man. He was a Volunteer Fireman stopping by to check his schedule who suggested that, since what was filling the foyer consisted mainly of water, if the water was turned off, so might the problem. And so the water to the building was cut and the flood seemed to abate, at least in the eyes of the few people watching. Most of the occupants had departed the offices in favor of the Police Department which offered them two things; one of which was a fire door between them and the rapidly filling foyer and it's attendant odor. The other, perhaps immediately more important thing, was that none of them had actually left the building, so it wasn't like they weren't at work. Got to keep an eye on those jobs.

But the flood wasn't abating. If anything it was picking up momentum, and with the Women's room door propped open, little chunks of big turds began rolling in arcs, stopping now and then

116

when they got too far off course to change direction back with the flow toward the foyer. Interwoven with these chunks were the inevitable wads of toilet paper, now slightly decomposed. And sanitary napkins, which demonstrated that not all the women who said they didn't flush them were telling exactly the truth, nevertheless if those things could not only go down once but also survive the return trip then obviously they've been flushable all along. The best one was the condom that slithered across the floor, rolling and folding and pointing the way to it's second hole of the day, to end up semi-floating in a question mark pose.

The water was turned off and the flood wasn't abating. That wasn't right.

"The Hell you think this shit is coming from?"

"Once through an asshole and twice through the toilets, moron!"

Working under these conditions tends to bring out less than the best in a person. Working in these conditions tends to graphically display to all the worst that has already come out of a person.

"No, I mean the water. There ain't any reason for it. I shut it off myself"

"All of it? All three valves?"

"What 'all three valves'?"

"Okay. You go find a mop and bucket. I'm going to finish shutting off the water."

The first building to be built in the complex was the Fire House. That was Phase One. Once the gas station on the corner was condemned under "Eminent Domain", progress on the Muni and it's magnificent sewer system began. Phase Two. The Library was built as Phase Three, but twelve years after the other two had been completed. There wasn't any particular hurry to make a new Library because the old one, although small and out-dated, did exist. So first a water line was built for the Fire House, but because it was a long way from the central water main to the place of need, only one three-inch line was put in. Once the Muni was up and ready, the three-incher for it was found to be more conveniently placed several hundred feet farther down the water main to allow for pressure drop. Look at a fire-sprinkler system in a building and you'll notice that

117

the diameter of the feed line decreases at each sprinkler head. Same principle; maintaining equal pressure down the line. If they were to have set it up so that all three valves were in the same place it would have cost at least fifty grand just for the sake of appearances. One valve was in Ligature Park, one valve was in the middle of the driveway where the tour busses unloaded, and one valve was contained within a concrete tomb under a foot of planting soil in a flowerbox at the Southeast corner of the Library. You had to know where to look in order to find them.

It was Children's Day at the Library, which meant a constant stream of restless kiddies heading for the can. Tiny tinkle, giant flush. Tiny turd, giant flush. The water hadn't been turned off there, yet, either.

Once a bucket is filled, whatever is filling it goes elsewhere. Such was how it went with that which was filling the Municipal Building. Out in the parking lot, things were not looking quite so fortunate.

*   *   *   *   *

"You can't tell the difference between having the Flu and being hung-over."

"Mr. Swanson, I have not had any more to drink than the one sip of scotch I had at your house last night, and excuse me for saying so but I don't think that's any of your business."

"Bill, it is very much my business when it concerns the welfare of this town."

It didn't matter a pair of coyote's kidneys whether or not Bill stayed, and Eddie Swanson knew it. Nobody was going to be inside this building for more than another hour at the most, and it didn't matter how quickly they got the foyer pumped dry. The whole building was going to stink until the carpet and panelling were replaced, and if they started right now and worked around the clock it would be well into next week until the place would be inhabitable again. And the town wouldn't pay the overtime for workers around the clock.

"I don't know what's gotten into him lately," Bill said to his secretary as he re-entered his office. His secretary wasn't listening.

118

She was at her desk, but she was wearing her coat, holding her purse with one hand and a handkerchief over her face with the other. The office was upstairs and at the opposite end of the building from the foyer, but the central air system had removed that advantage. The cover had been put over her typewriter in anticipation of the inevitable but she was a trooper and would stand her ground as long as she was needed. "I don't know what's come over him lately," Bill continued almost to himself, "but in less than a month he's alienated almost everybody he knows and lost the respect of the Town in the process. He seemed to change overnight, and he changed before Loughlin's death. If memory serves me, he changed about the time he brought that damned rock into his office."

*   *   *   *   *

"Basketballs? Fucking basketballs?

"Five of them. The longest stick I could get into the Culvert wasn't more than four and a half feet long and I was going to use it to push the basketballs farther up the pipe, but as full as I had them pumped it didn't do any good."

"What did you do to push them up?" Basketballs. I started laughing at this point, and it got to be almost convulsive, and that got Tony going. The sort of laughing that comes with a particularly good doobie followed by an equally good joke. It took a while, but he was able to get out the rest of the story in his own sporadic way.

"I let all the air out before I got there so they'd make a smaller package to carry. Getting that lid off wasn't bad, but putting it back in place was a bitch. I mean, there wasn't anything to pry against except the top wrung of the ladder and I didn't remove the lid with that in mind. But I got it back in place and had a room with a Pee-you." His little pun caught up with him and I took the time to trot down the hall to the can. I had been laughing so much I was about to wet myself anyway. By the time I got back Tony had calmed down to the point he was almost coherent, and he had proven himself able to fetch us each another beer. "So I folded each one to get it through the bars, then pumped it up as tight as it would go, and shoved it with my foot into the pipe as far as I could. Then I did the same thing with the next one, but it wasn't as easy with the

119

second one because they made a tight seal and got harder to shove with each one I put in. I don't know if the last one did any good because I couldn't do any more than inflate it against the bars, but it made me feel good putting it there so there is were it went."

Tony stopped talking at that point and just looked at me as though I was expected to say something, so I said something.

"Yes?"

"Yes!"

"And?"

"And!"

"And what?" Come on, Tony. You're saving something.

"And I figured that whatever I did with those basketballs wouldn't go unnoticed, but there was just too much potential within the bowels of that culvert" (a short snicker and a little snot. Indians aren't known for their puns, at least not in English.) "so with a little advance planning I decided that the outlet from the Culvert down to the Water Treatment Plant had to have a plug of it's own."

"You stuffed basketballs there, too?"

"No, they'd never fit. That's a fifteen inch line, and the only ball that would fit there would be a beachball. With the rough surface of a concrete pipe, the half-life of a beachball would be about zilch-point-shit. I needed something that would close it off well, would be water-proof, and would be cheap."

"I take it you gave this 'additional orifice' some extra thought?" What unmarried guy doesn't?

"Yup. A lot of it, and then it came to me. Sort of like the Jitterbug; so simple it damned near evaded me." Tony was never one to avoid plagiarism in order to make his point. "You've seen that foam-in-a-can stuff that you squirt into walls to keep out the cold or the heat or the flies? You unplug the push-button and shove a four-penny nail into the hole then slam the can down, nail first. The nail squirts-out and so does the foam-stuff. That's when you sling the can as far down the sewer pipe as it will go and let it do it's work."

"Enlighten me, Tony. I've got the idea, but as far as my imagination will go I want to know what really happens."

"The foam swells, and while it's swelling it sticks to anything it touches, even water."

"It doesn't stick to water."

"It doesn't need to. It squeezes the water out and sticks to where the water was. And what it doesn't stick to, it compresses against. It fills a lot of room, and it waterproofs what it fills. If I figured it even somewhat close, that sucker is going to back-up from several directions and it should take them enough time for at least several gallons of sewer-sludge to leak onto Main Street before they get it figured out. I think I did it right, and I did it in Po's name. Jesus, she was a dumb dog, but her heart weighed more than she did."

"Brilliant. Absolutely brilliant. And so bloody stupid! They ever catch you they'll hang you by your balls, and from the way you smell you'd better be wearing an industrial-strength jock strap. How long you been toting that odor?"

"Since around four this morning. That's when their guard is down."

"You didn't go back to the reservation and change clothes?" There wasn't a shower there at The Oliver's front yard, but he must have kept some clothes there.

"No, I can't be absolutely sure I wasn't spotted by somebody who might not say anything until they see what's happening today, so as soon as I climbed out of the sewer I cruised."

"Where did you spend the night?" I almost regretted the question before I asked it.

"You ought to keep more beer down there. Sometimes your friends get in late and thirsty." Oh, my poor sleeping bag!

"Why don't you jump in the shower and toss your clothes in the wash. I have some sweats you can wear until the dryer's done."

"Thanks, Jimmy, you're okay." About half way down the hall he turned around and very quietly said, "Buford didn't need to shoot her. She shouldn't have died."

Chapter Ten

The Rocky Mountains are blessed with the wealth of rivers and streams and creeks and lakes and ponds, and those waters attract fishermen from around the world. With worms and grubs and grasshoppers, with cheese and eggs and gooey green stuff that comes from Arkansas, with flies and nymphs wet and dry, sportsmen challenge the waters born of the glaciers and snowfields high above the timberline. Whether sitting on the bank or wading in rubber pants or scooting-about in a boat, when fishing in the Rockies the waters created their own music, their own reward. Such beauty, such grace, such, as Tony Engleman was so fond of saying, a bloody waste of time. The method used by Tony Engleman was none of the above.

Tony had been spending a lot of time with The Reverend Simms and his flock, sharing their "Sacramental Wine" at night and their "Sacramental Coffee" the next morning. He enjoyed their company, and even found himself able to sit attentively through the daily Sermons, both of them, whenever he was around. Tony wasn't "getting religion" any more than he had ever "had religion", at least not religion in the commonly accepted Judeo-Christian definition of the word, but Tony's a good listener and he simply preferred the company of these people over his Indian Brothers. His Indian Brother's attorney, John Chism, was with his People at least once a day to boost moral and bring in groceries and tell them all about the progress their cause was making, which was nice but it wasn't interesting. His Indian Brothers, and now also some of his Indian Sisters, had doubled in both number and gender and were all law students Chism had recruited to fill the extra tipis they'd found, but they weren't interesting. They mostly read their text books and debated the things that law students debate and every night the "Sisters" left the Oliver Property to have dinner in the home of a local sympathizer to bathe and sleep between warm clean sheets. John Chism had made that arrangement for them partly because none of the chicks could shit behind a rock, but also because he had the feeling that if the rumor got going that there was any "tipi-creeping" going on it could do irreparable damage to "The Cause". Since Tony was neither a scholar nor a celibate he soon found himself gravitating toward the flock of Rev. Simms with an increased frequency. He had also found a little part-time work. He'd been busted once for vagrancy, and with the attention he'd been getting from Buford lately he didn't want them to have any excuse to do it again. It also made him feel good about having something to chip into the collection plate that Rev. Simms didn't bother to pass but kept near the door, just inside the tent. Just inside the tent is where I ran into Tony for the first time in over a week.

"Dude! I'm surprised to see you here. Well, I came here to find you, so I can't be that surprised, but I didn't really expect to. I was just over to the Reservation and nobody there admitted to even knowing you."

"'Monsignor Dude' to you, Bitch, and no, they don't know me. Part of that's because they're all new from when we started, and part of that's 'cause I haven't introduced myself to them."

"Laying a little low these days?"

"No, not particularly. I'm just waiting for it to blow over before I get involved again."

"Again?"

"Po's still dead, isn't she?"

"Tony, they ever catch you, they're going to lock you in a room and throw away the room."

"Look, Jimmy, they've been trying to do that all my life. Every time there's a burglary in town I get questioned about it, but I've never done a B&E. Never. I can't keep a car because whatever I drive always ends up getting towed-away. My cars are traditionally uglier than a sack of assholes, but if you could lock somebody in jail for being ugly we wouldn't have had a President since Kennedy. They don't need a reason to hassle me, so now just because they have a reason but don't know it, it shouldn't make them act any different."

"You want to know how to stop them from harassing you? How many times have you had your license pulled for driving without insurance when you've had insurance? Twice?"

"Three times".

123

"And you've gone to court and proven you had insurance every time, right?"

"Yeah."

"So it's all a matter of public record. Do a little leg-work, get copies of everything you can put your hands on concerning those tickets and the Court proceedings and what they charged you to reinstate your license and what they charged you for impounding your car. Do the same for every bullshit bust you've ever had, and do the same for every time you've been wrong, too, just so there won't be any surprises. It's all a matter of Public Record so they can't hide it from you. If you stacked the bullshit on the left and the real ones on the right, which pile would be higher?"

"The left, of course."

"That's when you go to Denver and hire some shyster who works on commission. Won't cost you a cent, and you'll most likely get all your money back and a nice wad to boot. The worst that could happen is for you to let them know you're willing to fight back."

"The worst that could happen is The Town would crucify me."

"They're already doing that. Talk to John Chism. He'd at least let you know what your chances are."

"I don't know if this would be the right time to call a lot of unnecessary attention to myself."

"Think they suspect you?"

"I think that if they suspected me at all, Buford would be on me like white-on-rice. No, I just don't want my name to be fresh in their minds when they start making a list of most-likelies."

*   *   *   *   *

The tent had taken-on a new personality in the months since it had been first erected. There were, for example, no longer any Japanese lanterns strung outside. Mother Nature, or more specifically Mother Nature's gale-force winds which scream-down from the glaciers this time of year, had made quick work of them. They could have been reinstalled on the inside, but the little 1200 Watt Onan generator the local Christian Society had donated was

124

regularly putting out 75% capacity and there was no need to tax it to it's limit for some frivolous lights. There had also been donated a thick layer of sawdust on the floor that provided a softer place for feet to go than bare old burned concrete. It gave a layer of insulation against the frozen ground, and that was something Rev. Simms came to appreciate while he was standing at the Pulpit his Congregation had built for him. It was a nice Pulpit with a big comfortable dais upon which he could rest a Bible when he wanted to quote or his elbows when he just wanted to talk. As often as not, it was his elbows that did the resting. Made of aged "Barn Wood" planed smooth so that the subtle beauty of the natural patina remained, it's "elegant understatement" lending an air of dignity to the tent which pleased the Reverend Simms and his flock. For all it's outward appearance as your standard garden-variety Pulpit, though, it was unique in that it had only three feet to stand on. An observant member of the Pulpit-building crew had noticed that the concrete floor hadn't been laid with much care, probably because a wood floor was to be hung over it so finishing the concrete would have been a waste of time. Since three legs will balance but not wobble, three legs it was, with a small shim under one of the two front feet to make it reasonably level. The Rev. Simms liked the podium even though it had the tendency to tip backwards, which is one of the few "down" sides to a three-legged table. He learned to keep both elbows equally balanced on the edge of the Podium because if it was going to tip he wanted it to tip toward him so he could catch it, a feat he had already accomplished several times without anybody noticing.

The concrete floor should have been finished when it was poured, regardless of whether another floor was going to be suspended above it, and had the men who originally built it been qualified concrete workers rather than day-laborers they would have known why. Dragging a two-by-four across it's surface makes wet concrete look "good enough", but all of that tireless stroking and massaging with a batter-board does more than make it pretty and smooth. It brings water to the surface, and by doing that, three things are accomplished: First, the longer it takes for concrete to cure, the stronger the finished product will be. A thin layer of water on the surface of concrete goes a long way to insulate it against the heat of the day. When the water comes to the surface it brings with

125

it trapped air bubbles and sand. The air bubbles are self-explanatory, but the sand, by resting near the surface, forms a "shell", a hardened layer that gets the brunt of the abuse that concrete takes so well. This last and most important step hadn't been performed on the floor of the foundation of that building on the Oliver Hotel property, and that was probably what allowed the single rear leg of the pulpit to break through the surface of the concrete and almost go completely down and taking The Reverend Antione Simms almost completely with it.

There wasn't anyone else in the tent when it happened. Simms was leaning against the pulpit, first practising making eye-contact while mentally going over this evening's sermon, but eventually gazing nowhere in particular and reflecting on whatever crossed his mind. It didn't let go with either a bang or a whimper. It gave that hollow sound like when a head gets clobbered into a cupboard door, except without the consequential swearing.

Simms' first reaction was one of fear that he had broken the Pulpit. A lot of time and care had been put into it's making, and for him to break it in only a week's time would be an unseemingly awkward act for their Pastor. A little brushing-away of the sawdust with his shoe while he was still balancing the weight with his belly revealed what had really happened, and with a twist and a grunt he got the leg dislodged and swung out of the way. Nice hole. And deep, too. Take a bit of sawdust to hide that sucker.

Sawdust is good for covering but not for filling, and Rev. Simms knew that as soon as he saw just how deep the hole really was. It would need some real filling and before that it would need some cleaning. Good, for that would give him the opportunity to become "one" with this slab of pre-historic cement.

It hadn't been just a bubble under the floor. It was a bloody cavern, and where the Podium went through was only the tip of the iceberg. There was a good six-inch-wide swath of bedrock untouched by concrete exposed by the fist-sized hole, and he couldn't see how far it stretched in either direction. The men who laid this floor must have done it on Friday afternoon when they knew they were being laid-off on Monday morning. To do this patch right at least a lot of the existing concrete, certainly that on top of the crevasse, would need to be removed. Ah, well, it was Saturday afternoon and he could almost be guaranteed to have the place to himself because the majority of his parishioners would be out preparing themselves for a reason to attend Church on Sunday.

One thing about a Church, even if it is erected as a tent on ground well within the gray area of legality is that it is, nonetheless, a Church, and the inherent sanctity allowed any house of worship applies. The Church, any Church, be it St. Patrick's or a store-front Gospel, holds a particular power which keeps it from being ripped-off, and to this end the parishioners would sometimes keep tool boxes there over the weekend. Rummaging through the second box yielded a masonry chisel and a three-pound hammer. Another box held a pair of knee pads, those soft rubber things that kept you working on a lousy job; "San Francisco bedroom slippers", somebody had called them. That should do it.

It was important for The Rev. to collapse the remaining roof of the crevasse in order to avoid what had caused the problem in the first place, an air pocket, so he went to chipping away at the concrete. It was softer than he'd expected it to be, but after almost a century of alternately freezing and thawing we'd all be a little softer. It was so soft, in fact, that it was almost fun to chip away at it. Chipping concrete isn't fun under any circumstances, but this wasn't acting like concrete and was giving almost a retaliatory satisfaction in the name of any man who has ever tried to chip concrete by hand. Because of this, Antione Simms had gone farther than he had planned to go and was into the bedrock before he realized it but the journey had felt good. Sitting back on his haunches he began clearing the rubble: Chunk of gray concrete, little gray pebbles; chunk of gray concrete, fleck of yellow; chunk of gray concrete, lots of dust. A vacuum cleaner would help a lot with this stuff. There used to be a whisk broom around here, somewhere. Rumor has it that there used to be gold around here, too. I wonder if this is what they were talking about?

The sawdust made a beautifully removable camouflage for the crevasse that had began to appear in the concrete. "Under the pulpit and through the pews, to Grandfather's gold we go ...". The Reverend Antoine Simms had a streak of larceny in him about an

127

inch wide and almost yellow, like a touch of that black humor we all share which makes a Laurel and Hardy skit so incredibly funny. The Reverend Antoine Simms found a lot of humor in what so many now thought was so serious and nobody knew about two months ago. Nobody except me and someone else, and although I'm guessing at the "someone else" part, it seems pretty obvious by now that there was one. Probably still is one, but I just don't have a clue who he or she might be.

Truth be known, Rev. Simms landed on that particular concrete slab purely by accident. He went to the property on purpose, erected the tent where he did on purpose, but the slab merely represented his best chance of keeping his feet dry and his toes from freezing. Had he known that by being there and thereby denying "somebody" from having access to it, had he known just how far "somebody's" shrivelled testicles had crawled up his spine when he learned that Simms and his "little band of religious imbeciles" had parked their asses on his land, Simms would have split his gut laughing. As it turned out, he only got bits and pieces of the story about the gold one at a time so it took him several weeks of occupancy to put it all together. Once put together, he mused a while on the prospects and then forgot about it because the only reason he was here, truly here, was to clear a little space in his living room. Well, if in clearing that living room he also resurrected a little known Colorado statute, wasn't his life's work devoted to The Resurrection? A small pun on his part, but nothing sacrilegious. Now that he'd cleared the space in the living room he never got to see it more than the two or three times a week he went there to shower. That would need to change pretty quick, though, because a couple of his sermons had turned as sour lately as the mood of the town, and that had the same effect on his body odor. The whole town seemed to have turned sour lately. That was showing it's positive side by increasing his congregation slightly, but he was doubting if his talks got through to as many people. They weren't coming *to* him anymore as much as *for* him, which should be the ultimate goal of any "Sky Pilot", but something was definitely lacking. Oh, well, he'd leave that to the ones who'd started it. He still had Tony, and Tony, at least, had several reasons to be in the general vicinity most of the time, between his Native Amigos and dinner in the tent, so perhaps it wouldn't be out of line to ask him to keep an eye on the tent a little more often.

It was "keeping an eye on the tent" on Saturday that got Tony to go fishing. Tony, should anyone ever pose the question, doesn't fish. He explained it to me thoroughly one day while I was showing-off my newly acquired carbon-fiber, omni-flexible, hyper-balanced, ultra-grip trout-master:

"I don't fish."

* * * * *

The local Native Americans held, for the most part, what are considered today to be "Traditional Family Values", in that the men would forage for game while the women tended the home. Foraging for game might sound like a lot of fun to a guy who spends most of his life working a loading dock by day and coming home to the same double-wide at night, but when foraging is what you do for a living it takes on a new prospective. It is dirty, dangerous, back-breaking labor that goes unrewarded more often than it pays off, and if it goes unrewarded too many times in a row you and your family will starve. To this end, foraging was taken very seriously. In the Estes area there was abundant game in the nearby hills, but even then it was necessary to gather most of the game for the year during the warm months. Not unlike the way we earn most of our year's wages during the warm months today.

The women, staying in camp, didn't just run a day-care center. All of these people, men and women, had their share of social moments, but nobody underestimated the need to work as a team, as a tribe, in order to have the greatest chance of making it through the winter. Women gathered nuts and berries and grains to be dried for the ensuing months, and they tanned the hides and butchered and dressed and cured the meat that the men brought in. Everyone worked his butt-off toward a single purpose. Everyone, that is, except the kids. The kids wanted to romp and play and be kids, and this was not only tolerated but encouraged. There was one thing the kids could do to help stock the food supplies, however, that the adults didn't have time to do, and that was to catch fish. Fish are a small prey, a little mouthful for a lot of time, but not something to

129

be ignored while stocking the larder, so fish became the traditional "children's" quarry, and the children wasted no time getting the art of gathering fish down to a fine science. The kids, being kids, wanted to do anything other than what was expected of them. So they figured out how to get fish, a lot of fish, out of the water in the shortest period time, and they passed the method from older child to younger child, from generation to generation. What they did was make a small net from reeds or grasses and a long stick. Creep up to the bank of a stream where the bank has been undercut by the water, but never, never let your shadow touch the water. That's the big secret, because the fish can't necessarily see you but your shadow on the creek bed will make them freeze. Okay, you're at the edge of the bank, no shadow, and net in hand, right? Now *Stomp* the bank with your feet. The startled trout will dart a couple of feet away from the bank to see what's going on and it doesn't take much practice to bring the net up from behind and have them in the basket. A lot of fish in a little time.

Such was the method of Tony Engleman. Tony doesn't go fishing; Tony takes fish. A lot of fish in a little time. Something his older brother had shown him how to do. Tonight he had decided to "take fish" for The Church. He wasn't ignoring the Native Americans just a few hundred yards away, but they didn't need it. They had gotten a lot of good press lately, some of which had trickled-down to The Church, and that had manifested itself in some healthy support, none of which had trickled-down to The Church. Tony didn't view the situation as having a good side or a bad side, and, indeed, it hadn't crossed his mind that there might be "sides" at all. It was just that The Church needed him more than The Tribe, so that's where he was. Besides that, The Church was more interesting. The Tribe was doing well and eating well and making good progress, and that was more than Tony could have hoped for, so he allowed himself to be counted among their numbers but hung out at The Church. That's where he was when I caught up with him.

"Maybe I'll sue the Town later. It'll be too late for fish after dark, and I promised Trout for dinner so I got to get scooting."

"Aren't Trout maybe just a little unseasonable this time of year?"

"Jimmy, you ain't my momma."

"I'm sorry it sounded like that, Tony. I didn't mean it to. Besides, from what you've told me about your momma, she'd encourage you to snag something out of season now and then just to keep your hand in. I'm just thinking that if The Man sees you by the river it would give him a reason to want to talk."

"He don't need a reason."

"I know, but if ..."

"But if Karen Carpenter had eaten Mamma Cass's last sandwich, they might both still be alive. It's not that big a deal. I promised Trout for tomorrow. Judy's going to bake some bread and we're going to make it a 'Loaves and Fishes' sort of thing. You mind hanging out while I'm gone? Reverend Simms always feels better when somebody's here when he get's back."

"Sure. Where'd he go?"

"Just home for a shower. He should be bopping-in soon, but the Trout won't wait."

"Nothing to it, Buddy. I have to be at work by four thirty, but I can hang for a while. Good luck with the fishing."

"I don't fish."

With that he was gone, just he and his net and his gunny sack. The dinner he'd promised wasn't until after tomorrow's Service but the fish would stay fresh overnight this time of year and I had the feeling Tony had plans for the morning which didn't include stomping on the stupid bank of some stupid creek. The noise might be too much for him, as hung-over as he'd probably be.

I was alternately watching the clock and the VCR, not wanting to be late for work but not wanting to miss much of "The Stooges", either. The humor of "The Stooges" is sophomoric to say the least, but it is timeless. I don't think that it would be surprising to hear folks bitch about the sophomoric level of their humor a hundred years after the last of "The Stooges" had died.

John Chism poked his head in the tent. "Antoine in?" He and The Reverend Simms had early come to an agreement about the use of titles with each other. John Chism would call him Antoine if Antoine would drop the "Mr. Native American Counselor Chism" and just refer to him as "John". It pleased both of them in that by doing so there was never any attempt on the part of either to undermine the validity of what the other was doing. Actually, they

131

quickly began to complement the other's cause so while they were "independent entities" from their inception, the two leaders had become close friends.

"Hi, John", I said while I pried myself off the pew to shake his out-stretched hand. "I expect him back soon, or Tony told me I should expect him back soon. Just improving my mind with a video. Care to join?"

"Sure. What you been up to?" We hadn't visited much since the first day I met him, but I ran into him often enough so that we sort of knew each other and had a mutual respect based upon nothing other than a mutual respect.

"Working, mostly. Building an interest in local social developments."

"I thought I'd shit myself when Tony flooded the Muni", he casually offered as he sat.

"Who said Tony did that?"

"Tony. We couldn't bury his dog on the hotel grounds, but we did put up a monument and he got melancholy in front of it a few days ago and related the tale. Even told us about the Budweiser you keep under your house."

"Shit."

"Yup. Now I suppose he's gone fishing?"

"Tony doesn't go fishing."

"I know. He 'takes' fish. So do my nephews. Is that where he went?"

"That's what he told me, but you know Tony." Why did he have to open his big mouth? Not about coming to my house afterwards; that won't hurt me and if it did I couldn't be incriminated for anything unless the "Power's That Be" wanted me incriminated. They make their own rules.

"Say", John went on, "what's 'The Rev' doing here to make money? He sent word that he has this plan to buy the Hotel and wants to know if I want in on it. You hear anything?"

"No, but I rarely see him. I've got to get out of here pretty quick in order to make work on time. Why don't you stick around and ask him? I got to go. I'm interested in what he has to say."

"I'll keep you posted."

With that I was gone, but as I headed down toward PIGIRON, Simms was headed up.

"Jimmy! We're going to have a feed after the service tomorrow. Care to join us?" Always the benign recruiter.

"I'll try." My Sundays aren't regimented, but I have developed a pattern for them that I enjoy. Run to the store for dog-nuts and the paper, but the New York Times Crossword wont rot on the table until I get to it so maybe I would show up. "John's in the tent waiting for you." And with that I left. What the Hell were the Police chasing this time to make so much noise with their sirens?

*   *   *   *   *

"John. Glad to see you. I'd like your advice on something, but it must be kept absolutely confidential and I don't want you to be put on the spot. You want to hear?"

"Talk to me, Antoine. Lawyers are known for their ability to be discrete."

"That's what I've heard. You've know about the gold that's supposed to be on this property? What if I told you that I found it? What would be my chances of keeping it?"

"First off, don't tell me you found it. Your chances of keeping it, if you did find it which you didn't, approach the null set so forget that. There is no gold. With that in mind, what do you want to talk about? How much have you got?"

"About a gallon so far, and I haven't found any, remember? I want to buy this property for The Church. How do I do it?"

"A gallon of gold?"

"I've just about filled a gallon bucket with chunks I've scraped out from between the rocks. I don't know what it weighs because I can't lift it, but to make a rough estimate figure there are eight pints to a gallon."

"I'd say that was a fairly close estimate."

"Right. My Grandmother used to say 'a pint's a pound the world around', and she was right. A pint of water weighs about a pound, but that's a pint of water. A pint of pure gold weighs over nineteen times as much. Nineteen times eight pints equals one hundred fifty two pounds." His eyes twinkled as he held out the

133

piece of paper from which he was reading. "I had a little free time and used a calculator. One hundred fifty two pounds times sixteen ounces per pound equals two thousand four hundred thirty two ounces. Figure I take a real beating and can get only three hundred dollars per ounce, that yields slightly more than three quarters of a million dollars. How do I convert gold into acreage?"

"You don't, unless you can verify a benefactor to your Church, somebody with the assets to buy and the desire to do so. The question will be asked. Whoever buys this place will have their monetary lineage traced to the satisfaction of whomever wants to trace it and then they'll be challenged. Think of it as sort of like when the Feds do something spectacular, like a major denial. Most Law Students are looking to get a Law Degree and then do their best to be worthy of it, but some of them want to be remembered as Chief Justice John Marshall and figure that a spectacular case will be a shortcut down the path. Everybody thinks that the Feds are always trying to be tricky, but they have so many watchdogs tracing everything they do that you could be hard-pressed to find a more straight-up pile of paranoids than those who make the big decisions. That's why, to over-simplify it, you can have such a bitch of a time renewing your driver's license. And they'll expect the same thing from you. Why do you ask?"

"What I visualize is a viable 'Grand Old Hotel' dedicated to three things. Most importantly, it will be one of the last of the 'Grand Old Hotels' left in the United States. Modern history has shown us that such an entity cannot support itself in today's economy, so that makes me think that it must be diversified in behalf of it's own support."

"Of course it must be diversified. That's why ninety percent of the Hotel's property had to be sold over the last twenty years to pay the Hotel's bills. It has no choice other than to diversify, now that it's all gone."

"Listen to this, John. You have an interest in this property. What that interest is verses the interest you have in promoting your cause is irrelevant. It looks to me as though I can come up with at least half-again as much money as I have without lifting too many eyebrows. How do you suggest we funnel it into the Hotel?"

"A partnership might help fog the situation for a while, but don't count on anything other than the truth to stand the scrutiny of a dedicated researcher, and that isn't always good enough. And what do you mean 'we', White Man?"

"I mean you as an entity and me as an entity. Your Native American Research Center, and my little Church. I don't know what the tax situation is with you, but my line of work offers some hefty 'bennies'."

"It might work, and I might be able to work with you on it. What, specifically, do you have in mind?"

"Something for The Church, something for the Native Americans, something for the Tourists who will ultimately support the place, and something to earn a living for the Hotel."

"How do you expect to launder the money from the gold?"

"I really hadn't thought about it as 'laundering'."

"What would you call it?"

"I guess 'laundering' is a pretty good word after all. I hadn't really thought about it too much other than to want to ask somebody who might know about such things. I've got a bucket of gold I want to trade for a hotel. How can I do it?"

"Let me look into it. I have a friend who specializes in Securities who may have an idea."

The conversation was cut short as one of the Law Students burst into the tent.

"John," he gasped, out of breath from sprinting over, "we need you right away."

"What's up?" he asked as he rose from the Pew.

"Tony's been shot!" And with that, the Student was out the tent-flap door and gone.

"Who did it?" John called behind him as he went through the door.

The Reverend Simms had remained seated during the brief exchange, but he could hear their raised voices as they headed back to their camp.

"Buford did it, the same fucking cop that shot his dog!"

Chapter Eleven

"Of course I'm carrying a gun."

Just because I hadn't seen Pauli for several months didn't mean that I had expected him to call. We'd arranged to meet for a late lunch in the lounge at the Holiday Inn, and that surprised me a little. In Estes Park what isn't immediately obvious is the presence of one restaurant or bakery or hot dog stand within the town limits for each four dozen of the permanent residents, and with that in mind selecting a cookie-cutter chain doesn't make a lot of sense and is almost never done by the locals. Not that the Holiday's so bad, but you can go to any large town and most small ones and nibble the same stuff, so the locals will generally opt for one of the more creative eateries, and those we pick are the ones which are the most consistent. Like Vern's restaurant up the hill toward the old A&W where you can get a vegetarian meal that actually has flavor, or Fat Sam's Barbecue in the middle of town where you can get anything but a vegetarian meal, and both places have Budweiser on tap.

The Lounge at the Holiday Inn isn't what anyone who stays out later than six in the evening would call a "destination bar", but it is clean and not too pricey and has three televisions. Pauli was staying in the hotel which meant that not only had he beaten me to the bar but from the scraps of used groceries scattered around the shadow of his empty plate he'd also gotten a jump on lunch. His coat was bulging like it was the first time I met him and it seemed a little conspicuous for an ex-cop to be carrying a gun and, considering the atmosphere in town, that could be the sort of thing you might want to keep to yourself no matter who you are. So of course that was the first thing I brought up.

"I didn't think you were still licensed for it."

"Are you waving The Flag at me, becoming a 'Concerned Citizen'? I never knew you to get hung-up on technicalities, Jimmy. What you going to do next, hug a tree?" Pauli hadn't asked me to meet him so that we could exchange idle banter. From the looks of the chicken bones he'd gnawed-clean he hadn't asked me for lunch, either. I ordered a Bud and a plate of Buffalo Wings from Chuck behind the bar, then prepared to engage in small talk until Pauli was ready to get down to business. He didn't stall or beat around the bush, but Pauli was a cop, or at least he used to be, and badge-blood runs deep. Once I'd answered the questions he didn't ask, he'd get around to asking the questions for which he didn't need answers. He was on a mission, like a shrewd Southern Businessman who dresses in shabby clothes to drop the guard of his adversaries and plays "The Good Old Boy" for their amusement and his profit.

Pauli had glided back into town once again. A calming force. Glad to see him. Wonder what he's up to? He'll tell me when he's ready, and if I change the subject and he comes back to it, that means he's ready.

"Where's the Jag?" Some cars are conspicuous by their absence, and a Black-On-Black-On-Black Jaguar Coupe could redially be counted among them.

"Sold it. My insurance came up and it was the down-payment on a new Dodge. A Dodge ain't a Jag, but at least I can afford to drive one."

"I always thought that once you bought a car like that, little annoyances such as insurance were to be expected if not tolerated. Didn't you project the cost of keeping the car as an original part of the price of the car?"

"When did you last own a Jaguar?"

"I drive PIGIRON, and that's about as happy as I get."

"Case closed, Jimmy. If you ever have the opportunity to boast that you once owned a twelve-cylinder, Leather-and-Walnut appointed, one hundred and sixty mile-per-hour car,

137

you will consider it, by hind-sight, to have been one of the finest investments of your life. The second year of ownership translates into trading it in for a tall stack of dollars and a new Dodge."

"It's a nice Dodge", I said, trying not to sound condescending.

"A '48 Plymouth looks like an interesting drive and I wouldn't mind doing it on occasion, but there's a reason cars are made the way they are today. You have an eighty-five mile-per-hour car. You ever take it to eighty-five?"

"It don't think it would do eighty-five in a free-fall, but for the sake of argument let's say it could. I've never had it above around fifty."

"How does it drive at around fifty?"

"I think that's when it enters it's element and becomes 'one' with the road."

"I've kissed a hundred-and-fifty in the Jag a couple of times, and while there's no adrenalin rush I've ever had like it while I was behind a wheel, I truthfully didn't care for it. Cars like that are made to go fast, but they're not made to stop fast or flip fast, so if I'm not going to use the potential, why pay for it?"

"Because, Pauli, an old Plymouth is a lot of fun and a new Dodge is a nice drive, but a Jaguar is 'Pussy'." He was right of course, but seemed to be in a jocular mood so I thought I'd push it just a little.

"A stud like me gets all the pussy he can use on his swarthy demeanor and debonair disposition alone, and I could drive a rusted 1961 Rambler Ambassador Station Wagon and still need to turn-away the Babes." I could tell he was getting into the spirit of the conversation.

"Sure you could, if the trailer you towed behind you had a sign on it that said, 'Caution: Penis On Board'."

I could see the direction this conversation was going, and while I don't make a habit of engaging in "locker room" talk, this conversation was becoming enough fun I didn't want to drop it yet. Evidently, Pauli did.

"You know, Jimmy, from the moment you get born you're playing a game against the odds," he began. I can never tell whether he is gathering information or having a pleasant chit-chat. "It isn't you against anyone or anything other than yourself, and everyday you stay alive the odds get stacked against you just a little higher. The older you get, the more friends you've lost, the closer attention you pay to the odds."

"Is this about Tony?"

"Yeah, it's about Tony, and it's about your father and my both of my brothers and everyone else we've outlived at too young an age to have done so. It isn't about being fair or right or just, because none of those things have anything in common with life."

"I haven't felt immortal since the first time I was in Viet Nam."

"That's when you stopped being a kid. Immortality is an extravagance reserved for kids; it's their domain and once they step out of that domain, once they stop being kids, they may never reenter 'The Kingdom'. I believe I'm going through a delayed mid-life crisis, so death has been on my mind lately and that's what I think about when my mind wanders. You okay with Tony?"

"No, of course I'm not okay with Tony." Asking if you're 'okay' with a tragedy is a bullshit nomenclature that allows a friend to simulate emotional involvement without becoming emotionally involved. "Tony got dead when he shouldn't have been dead by a cop who shouldn't have been a cop. There's nothing I can do about his death and there's nothing that will be done about the cop, but there is something that ought to be done to stink-up this town a little. I'm not okay with Tony, and right now I want somebody to pay." I could feel my mood changing for the worse and I wasn't doing much to hide it from Pauli.

139

"Jimmy, when you were in the Navy, you ever bitch about your ship?"

"It was a way of life."

"What if somebody else bitched about your ship?"

"I saw a couple of bars in Subic Bay get pretty trashed because of it. One even got burned to the ground, but that probably had as much to do with a bad blow-job as a ship."

"That's a little extreme, wouldn't you say?"

"I don't know. We were all shuttling between Subic and 'Nam, sometimes not having enough time to go ashore for six or eight weeks at a stretch, and when having the ship strafed by shore-fire is fresh in your mind there really isn't time for a bad blow-job."

"There ain't no such a thing as a bad blow-job."

"You were never in Subic Bay."

"Sounds like I didn't miss much. But bitching about your ship, that's the way it is with being a cop. When you're a member of The Force you can bitch all you want, but you get so tired of listening to civilians rag on what they don't know anything about that sometimes you want to do nothing more than get them to shut up about it. When a cop does that, everybody pays, and the only thing that can be done about it is to see that it doesn't happen again."

"Aren't you being a little bit simplistic about the situation, Pauli? Legislating morality has been tried before and will undoubtedly be tried again, but it will have no more success in the future than it's had in the past."

"The way you change a Police Force is to join it and change it from within."

"You planning on becoming Estes's oldest rookie?"

"In a round-about way, but they won't know I've been here until I'm gone."

"It shouldn't be too difficult to throw a blanket over the heads of those morons without them suspecting the lights went out, but how are you ...".

140

"I'm FBI."

I doubt that my jaw dropped or my eyes glazed-over or I broke into a sweat. I could, however, feel myself going numb. "Pauli," I said, "you just stopped being a cop. How much is enough? I mean, why not stay with New York City if you want to keep being a cop? Transfer to another Department or Section or whatever it is you guys do for a change of scenery."

"It's part of a special program the FBI set up to make themselves look better by improving themselves from within so that they are better."

"A little 'Image Enhancement' at the Federal level?"

"That's what I'm doing, and it not only has two rooky Feds scared shitless but also gives me jurisdiction anywhere I want jurisdiction. Those rooky Feds are going to end up better in their jobs."

"I'm glad to see you here. I always am. That out of the way, what the Hell you doing here? Just out of blind curiosity."

"I'm here in an 'Official Capacity', but that information is unofficial. I've met the Mayor-Pro-Tem once on a less-than-social occasion. Now I want to meet him officially, but by his official standards and not mine. I want him to want to see me."

"That shouldn't be too hard. He doesn't have many friends left and might enjoy a little company." My 'wings' had arrived and taking the razor edge from my hunger gave me the impetus to continue listening with an open mind.

"The FBI has been accused of many things since it's inception, and of those things incompetence rises most pointedly to the top, but the FBI has never, ever been accused of inside corruption. That's more than can be said for the last pile of cops I worked with, and that in and of itself makes me want to work with them and for them."

"You're an 'Idealist'," I laughed, "a bloody 'Idealist'. Next thing you're going to tell me is that you're a liberal. A Commie-Pinko, Bed-Wetting Liberal." This was getting to be too good to keep a straight face.

"And what," asked Pauli, breaking into a bit of a grin himself, "is so surprising about me having the common sense as to not walk such a narrow path like the one which might exclude any thoughts possibly construed as liberal?"

"Nothing is surprising about a middle-aged cop having any liberal thoughts at all. Why should you ask?" At that, I lost it.

"What did you do for Christmas this year, Jimmy?", Pauli inquired after the appropriate interlude required for me to get my act together.

"What? Christmas? I didn't do Christmas this year. In fact, I've rarely done Christmas. When I was a kid we were always broke, so we usually had an 'Anti-Christmas'.

"How does one go about an 'Anti-Christmas'?"

"You wait until everyone else goes to bed and then sneak around the house stealing what you want. When you wake up in the morning, what you've been able to keep is yours."

"You about ready for a drug test?"

"You about ready for a wet chin?" I don't do mandatory drug tests. In fact, it has long been my opinion that the only reason I'd do a voluntary Urine Analysis would be for a taste-test for the guy who invented it. Nor should there be hypochondriacs, stray dogs, homeless families, simpering bimbos, or Methodists.

"Jimmy, who do you think's in charge of the FBI? Today?"

"I don't know who's running the FBI right now and I don't care who's running the FBI right now, but I'd put money that who ever the sleazy weasel is, put a gun in his hand and he couldn't hit the barn side of a broad."

142

"Good. That's what I do for a living, trying to rebuild a losing image, and what you just said gives me job security."

"You're padding the bra of an adolescent administration, stuffing Kleenex into the ...".

"Now you're sounding like my former wife."

"You've never said you were married. You ever have any kids?"

"Of course I've never had any kids. I don't have a uterus." Peering over the side of his uplifted glass Pauli asked, "Where's Estes Park going from here?"

"Downhill, I'm afraid, but do you realize, Pauli, that you haven't said a word about Gold for over three months?"

"Yes I realize it, and I suggest strongly that you say nothing about it either."

"Why not?"

"Between you and me, there might be a couple of my new boys singing the Hallelujah Chorus right about now."

*   *   *   *   *

Tony's funeral hadn't been any great shakes, but neither was the Cemetery in which he was inturred. For years Estes Park had avoided a Cemetery because of the assumed adverse reaction that acknowledging death might have on the Tourists; this is a tourist town, a retirement town, and regardless that it entertained an abnormally large number of deaths it had long ago been deemed unfitting by the City Fathers to admit that many people came here to die. Once the Cemetery, privately owned, had been finally allowed it was certified at it's site for three very important and three very distinct reasons; location, location, and location. Immediately to the East was one of the finest institutions of it's sort in the Nation, if not the World, and what that institution taught was an dependency-free life without substance-abuse. Great place to set a Cemetery; right next-door to where you could expect to be if you continued your misfortunate ways. "Yonder lies the alternative", spake the Grim Reaper.

The next reason was, surprisingly enough, location. It, the Cemetery, became located on it's spot because that particular spot happened to be in one of the least travelled areas of the town, and certainly not somewhere a Tourist could find without the prior instructions necessary to satisfy an abnormally morbid curiosity.

The last reason for it's location was that it lie in one of the few bleak areas of town. In an area of glaciers and rivers and Pine Trees and all those other fiddly things associated with the Rocky Mountains it would be a difficult task at best to convince anyone from Iowa that this is an Alpine Desert. Perhaps it's not quite that, but I've found Prickly Pear Cactus growing native up here. Stunted, but native. Also something from the Family Mammilaria, plus a third which resembles an Ocotillo but couldn't possibly be one. An Alpine Desert. Scrub-land desert in the Rocky Mountains, and nobody'd believe it. We don't have rattlesnakes other than those which hitch-hike up the hill with a load of Alfalfa hay and the ones which do get her can't live through the Winter, but this area can be an enigma of perceptions. Sort of like Tony, an enigma of perceptions. But the land lay in a minor flood plain and wasn't saleable for much else, so the owner was allowed to turn it into a Cemetery in exchange for the Town receiving a right-of-way on another chunk of land owned by the same guy to whom they might have otherwise actually needed to pay something that rhymes with "money". It was suitable that Tony be laid to rest in a flood plain because with the next high water the fish could come to him, which made a lot of sense because Tony didn't fish.

Antione Simms had conducted the ceremony, of course, and had done it like the gentleman he was. He'd touched on Tony's positive qualities for a bit and let it go at that. Tony didn't need to be lauded in the eyes of his peers, if a person like Tony could be said to have had any peers, and the ceremony was kept short and sweet. When you get right down to it, nobody outside of the movies really wants to attend a funeral and nobody who was here this afternoon really wanted to be here this afternoon doing what they were doing, with the possible exception of Bufford. Bufford put it an appearance, but didn't get out of his Patrol Car. He didn't even shut off the engine, but that may have had to do more with the mourners than Bufford's original intentions. As soon as the Cop responsible for the ceremony being conducted was spotted driving near, three of the male members of the Congregation and one of the women moved in silent unison to a line parallel with the slowing car and perpendicular to the grave. Blocking the view of the ceremony from the now-stopped Patrol Car, this quartet had simultaneously dropped trou' and then, feigning embarrassment over the situation, they winked at each other and bent from the waist as one in order to retrieve their fallen britches. That they had each hooked their thumbs in each side of their drawers, those several of them who were wearing drawers, and that the undergarments followed their hands on the slow journey to their ankles was irrelevant. Bufford had been "mooned" during the funeral of the man who's life he'd taken. It isn't too often one has the opportunity to hear a round of a applause during a period of mourning, much less a hearty cheer, but as Buford stared in disbelief, the one woman of the chorus line farted while her head was near her knees in a manner which could only be described as a majestic passing. Having been said to be two axe-handles wide across the butt by the time she was in her early teens, summarized as having the appearance of two hogs fighting in a burlap sack any time she took one of her too-infrequent trots, Bufford witnessed the tremulous concussion of too much celulite and too many small red pimples flapping against each other in a ribald mockery of the San Andreas Fault earping odious fumes. That's when I got the idea, the revenge I could do for Tony that wouldn't include lawyers or murder.

The Cemetery is located on a couple of acres of land across the river from the fish hatchery. The hatchery had been setup in the mid-Twenties by a few local business men when there came to be enough visitors to the town that once several of those visitors were heard to grumble about not catching their limit in the first hour they went fishing, whichever hour of the day that might be. Because it was a private commercial venture and not originally government-funded, it cut the usually incurred corners of bureaucracy and did an efficient job of getting the fish from the growing-ponds to the river without all the mucking-about involved in being overly cautious. Those gates could be easily broken.

*   *   *   *   *

The Tucson Gem and Mineral Society was, during the late Forties and early Fifties, putting on a display of the collections of it's members once a year for the sake the general public. Presumably they still are, but I don't actually care and since it has nothing to do with The Greater Scheme Of Things I haven't bothered to check. What brings them into the conversation at all is that during that time a prospector-turned-miner was loading a rail car per month with ore, where it was then hooked onto a passing train and taken to the smelter. As he told the story, he was driving into Tucson one day and noticed a billboard advertising The Society's exhibition so, having some free time on his hands, he attended. Much to his surprise and eventual delight he found somebody selling his ore, ore that the seller had legally found spilled at the railroad siding, and selling it for two hundred times what it brought from the smelter. Realizing that a career-change was eminent, Gabe, the prospector, began to inquire what it would take to obtain a sales booth and was met with discouragement from the

146

people running the exhibit. He did eventually get a booth for the last day of sales to the public, but remained confused as to why there was such a problem in wanting to give these guys money for simply taking about forty square feet of the Fairgrounds. He didn't really need to be any closer than about thirty feet to them, yet they balked. After the show closed for the day, he introduced himself to several of the other eleven sellers and the rest of them introduced themselves to him. They agreed to meet for drinks in a couple hours at The Holiday Inn, which was at the time The Marriot, and what came out of that meeting changed the lives of those men; the "Dirty Dozen", as they came to call themselves in later life, in a manner in which even their wives of many years looked upon with a jaundiced eye. Although Gabe had only met these men that day he felt a special kindred toward them and their type in that they all wanted to earn a living by picking up a rock, toting it to town, and selling it for more than what it cost him to get it to the buyer. There are "Rock Shows" in the World which have their own music, and after many Jim Beams and a prestigious amount of Budweiser, these gentlemen decided that they would begin an equal but separate showing of different fashions of rocks and see what they could do with it. After all, they all loved their families, and they had assured themselves of that repeatedly until the bar shut down for the night.

When some of them awakened in the morning their terminal hang-overs had not quite taken their full measure of the man and they remembered what had been said the night before. The others needed to be carried from bed and coaxed into a cold shower in their pajamas. What they had proposed during their tumultuous drunken comradery was "that if these bastards want to allow sellers in but only enough of them to foot their bills, then these bastards are missing a hot lick by refusing to sell the stones to the people who want to buy them". So they agreed to start their own show, but this one would be geared to accommodate the fine folks who wanted to do nothing

147

more than shuck-out their hard-earned sheckles for a particularly attractive piece of the Planet Earth, and they would do it at a time of year which would coincide with the "other guys" show. The price of rent must have been going up too fast for some people even in the early Fifties. And the seller's Show grew and blossomed and then exploded, with each of the "Dirty Dozen" centralizing on a particular aspect of the Gem Trade; they divided the Show somewhat by the Mos Hardness Scale. Someone pursued Berylls and Corundums, known locally as Rubies, Emeralds, and Sapphires. Rubies and Sapphires are exactly the same stone except that Rubies are red and Sapphires are any other color in the range of clear to black. Find a clear or black Star Sapphire some time when you have nothing else to do for the afternoon. The hardness of Emeralds is significantly higher than the Beryls, but either stone is so significantly harder that anything other than Diamonds that it doesn't matter, and the nice part about hardness is the polish it will take. Nobody openly dealt in Gold because back then it was too tightly controlled by The Feds, but nobody wrote receipts for their sales, either. Play both sides of The Fed's game. One of the men was enamored with Turquoise, which is soft enough to be scratched by a fingernail. A fingernail and a copper penny are about equally hard, although tearing a penny is a rare-enough occurrence that is not generally a topic of social conversation.

What these guys had on their tables and the tables of the people renting space from them were the most gorgeous stones on the face of The Earth, and they all made a fortune selling to the people who wanted to buy such stones. Together, in twelve separate hotels, the "Dirty Dozen" put together on a drunken whim the world's largest and most successful Gem and Mineral Show, with each of the original entrepreneurs eventually retiring and passing the dream and the baton at his discretion. Some of the shows merged with each other, and what had begun on a small scale, the dream of a few men who began one company to make a living for their families while helping others make a living by selling rocks, was now a dream that had risen. They'd stuck to the concept, and the show grew and prospered and gained momentum year by year until today The Tucson Gem and Mineral Show requires the facilities of five separate hotels bulging at their seams with five separate displays run by five separate organizations, and there's more than enough business to go around. When Mick joined The Show, the company he worked for had already overrun both the basement and the entire first floor of the largest high-rise hotel in Tucson, and that accounted only for the dealers who chose to display their wares publicly. A large number of the dealers worked out of private suites in the upper floors of the hotel where they could have buyers drop by one at a time by invitation-only and then only under the close scrutiny of the seller's armed bodyguards. These guys are as serious as the merchandise they're selling, but when you have several billion dollars worth of rocks under one roof it pays to be serious. Mick got to know a few of the regular "upper-floor" men, the ones who came to the show every year, during the after-hours relaxing done in the lounge of the hotel. He liked most of them because when you get to their level in their business it doesn't pay to be sleazy, so after a day of hauling extension cords for the "slick" peddlers in the basement it was nice to immerse one's self in "honest" folks, and the ones he liked the most were the Afganis named Mohammed. All the Afganis were named Mohammed. They had explained that because it was the only Afgani name Americans could pronounce, and since it was seen by Afganis as an insult to have their names not pronounced correctly they were all named Mohammed, and they were dealing in the finest Lapus Lazuli in the World. In the early days of Mick's time with The Show they were funding a war against The Soviet Union, which meant they were in the habit of working with large sums of money by necessity. By the time the war ended, the large sums had become a habit with

149

them and they continued the practice, only now the sales were returning to their country in the form of cash rather than Surface-To-Air Mssiles. It was Mohammed who Mick sought out tonight.

"My friend", Mick began in that easy going manner that came so naturally to him, "there is a person in the hotel you should meet."

"Somebody interested in the finest Lapis, which is the finest stone in all the world, should pay closer attention to the clock. It is all locked away for the night."

"No, this doesn't have to do with Lapis. This is the gentleman my brother in Colorado told me about, the one I mentioned to you last night."

"Forgive my memory, my good friend Mick, but in my Country we are not allowed to drink alcohol. Attempting to put a year of 'social drinking' into the three weeks we are in The States does nothing to undermine the validity of my country's Religious Law. Who is this person?"

"Mohammed, I'd like you to meet The Reverend Antoine Simms. He is also an observer of Religious Law, and he has something much more valuable to you than your excellent Lapis or the dollars you receive for it."

$$* \quad * \quad * \quad * \quad *$$

Colorado, unlike many States, doesn't have a "fishing season", as such. Certain species are protected during certain months and some species are protected every month, but for all practical purposes most of the lakes and rivers are either frozen-over or the weather is just too damned cold during the gestation period of the eggs or when the fry need protecting that an enforced "season" isn't necessary. With a self-regulating season, fishing isn't really done on a grand scale until not only the rivers and lakes thaw and flow but the air warms enough for a sane person to be in it for a sustained period of time, if fishermen could be loosely grouped among the sane. With this in mind, State Fish Hatcheries gather roe and sperm when it's available and bring them together at the appropriate time convenient to both the growth of enough fish to appease the folks buying the licenses and the budget The State has begrudgingly poked at them which enables them to feed enough fish while growing to the required substantial size. During early February in Estes Park the growth of the next Spring's crop was well underway because the Fish Hatchery had long ago built-in a provision for maintaining a large stock of Prime Breeders. It was these select five hundred trout, these fish which were intended for a life of Piscine fornication-and-debauchery and never meant to grace the fetid bacon grease of some flatland-foreigner's frying pan, these were the stinking and bloated corpses which lined the riverbank that channeled the water which entered the Northwest end of the Town of Estes Park.

There is a chemical sold under the brand name of Rotonone which is a fine weapon in the arsenal in the war against the spread of disease and pollution. What it does is remove oxygen from water without contaminating the water itself; it dissipates into relatively nothing within a day or so, and everything within that body of water which relied upon oxygen for life would die but the next day the same species could be reintroduced germ-free and all would be nice and puff and clean. I didn't want to contaminate the ponds at the Hatchery and I didn't really want to kill the fish, but I got to thinking about what I had said to Pauli about "stinking-up the town" and it all came together. I'll probably have some very bad dreams about this in the future, but my attitude is that if Tony Engleman can't fish then neither can anyone else. Tony Engleman didn't fish.

Some people were aghast at the waste of life, but most people took the attitude that those fish were like the cows born to be ultimately ground into Big Macs; they wouldn't have been

151

born at all if it wasn't to supply a food source. Most people were aghast at the stench of a ton and a half of dead trout rotting in the middle of town, but some others observed that had it not been for the unseasonably warm weather which kept the rivers from freezing-over the whole thing could have gone unnoticed.

The merchants all noticed it. The rare shirt-sleeve weather just before Valentine's Day had guaranteed a banner year for sales, and now, when the stores should be full of shoppers bursting with 'Valentine's Love', the streets were nearly deserted. Lord, this town does stink. I wonder if Tony Engleman can smell it from where he's sitting? "Howdy, Tony, What do you think of the stench? You find 'Po yet? How's she doing? You ever get five bucks for her?"

*　　*　　*　　*　　*

'Wavy Davy' was at it again. He'd stopped being an Electronics Technician for the same reason as most of the people who leave that field; he got tired of "chasing electrons", but he hadn't discarded his knowledge along the way. He was currently, not to make a pun, washing dishes for a living while trying to design a Cobalt Bomb. So far he'd deduced that with about eighteen thousand tons of a particular type of small electric motor (previously discarded, of course, ergo within his budget) he could begin to develop the prime mover for his project. Wavy Davy wasn't stupid, just wavy, and the pursuit of possessing a "personal nuclear device" only served to keep him amused with the prospect of nuking the next person to piss-him-off, which would probably be the next person with whom he spoke. When you're a nerd and have been on the receiving end of nerd jokes for half a century there's a cynical air which develops around you concerning people who are not nerds. As often as not, this attitude will manifest itself into the sort of mental complex which justifies being a nerd due to superior

152

intellect. What came of this, in the case of Wavy Davy, was that when somebody made a snide comment about him and he got that silly smirk on his face, everyone who thought that his expression was due to his sense of humor was dead wrong. Or would be, if Davy had his way.

Short of a nuclear holocaust, which Dave recognized as a fantasy and not really one of life's alternatives, what he did know was that if a tone were to be reverberated between twenty and thirty thousand cycles per second all the dogs within earshot would bark, and that was a task which was within his grasp. Young children and women are able to perceive sounds at that level when grown men can't, and because Wavy Davy liked the ladies almost as much as they disliked him he'd need to be careful where he aimed it. Such a device is easily made from some resistors and capacitors and a cheap chip from Radio Shack. And a speaker of course, but speakers are cheaper than the chip if you know which dumpster the TV shop uses. A few transistor-radio batteries hooked in parallel could keep a low-draw speaker cooking for hours, if not days. That ought to work.

This tone-generation line of thought was getting to be fun; tone-generation can be your friend. What Dave wanted to do was create a minor diversion that would semi-cripple communications in town, build a little pandemonium, be a prelude to a nuclear holocaust, see how they liked it for a change. Why not? The time was right and so was the mood of the town. Getting all the dogs in town to bark was one thing, but that was only intended to spark tempers and add chaos to an already confusing situation.

If he was going to be the first on his block to rule the world through nuclear domination he would need to do it like the big boys do and take the enemy apart one piece at a time. In this case, it would need to be the Police who went down first because they would be the first obstacle in his way, and that should be pretty simple for somebody who was smarter than they were and probably smarter than the people who built their radios. That was the approach he planned to take; remove a cop's radio and you effectively remove the cop. What was going through his mind the last time anybody remembered seeing him is known in electrician's circles as a "Tank Circuit", the thing in a cordless telephone that generates the frequency of the signal between the handset and the base unit. What he was muttering to himself was that were he to couple one of those to a 'Class B' Push-Pull Amplifier stolen from a junk television he should be in business. A 'Buzz-Word' among the small circle of people who care about such things, a Push-Pull Amp could be set to turn a frequency $180°$ from it's normal transmission in order to make the TV picture's line of electrons sweep back and forth across the screen. The plan was so brilliant in it's simplicity that it couldn't fail. The Estes Park Police Department uses three radio frequencies for communications, and the main frequency was the only one to which the dispatchers had access; the other two were reserved for chit-chat between the patrol cars. Set the frequency of the "Tank Circuit" slightly to one side of the cop's frequency, broadcast a signal exactly opposite of that signal, and the cop's transmission would be negated. They could still hear but they couldn't talk, only they wouldn't know they couldn't talk. Davy's little transmitter wouldn't make any audible noise, just a frequency that would turn itself on when the cops tried to broadcast, and by being not tuned quite exactly to the police radio it would shut itself off automatically when the cops were finished with their idle pratter.

The main police frequency would be the easiest to take out because that antenna was stationary on the roof of the Municipal Building and there are many little nooks and crannies up there where the transmitter could be hidden. It would also be the most expensive because he'd need to make an invertor to change the 110 Volts of alternating current conveniently available on the roof to the 12 Volts direct current used by his transmitter, but nobody had ever said World Domination would come cheap. The transmitters he put on the police cars would be one of the car-to-car frequencies (no need to be redundant) and easier to hook up, but the risk involved in crawling under the cars in plain sight made that job a lot more dangerous. Oh, well, all that was necessary was to tape it to the car's frame and connect one wire to the battery via the starter motor, which was always hot, and the other wire to a good ground. Five minutes per car times six cars could get the job done on a lunch break, if he wanted to go to lunch at three in the morning on Monday. All the cops were home in bed at that time on that night, leaving the town in the capable hands of the County Sheriff, and the County Sheriff wasn't going to be keeping an eye on the local police cars.

Chapter Twelve

There were a dozen of them scattered on the hill above town, a loose confederacy of rock climbers who's singular mission was to make a two-word statement to the town and do it in a way that could not be misunderstood. Between them they had acquired, through quietly hustled donations, over two hundred dollars toward their goal, and that was enough money to buy a lot of thirty-minute highway flares.

The hill was a gentle slope that rose through the Ponderosa Pines for a half a mile before terminating abruptly at the cliff that molded the Southern limit of the Business District. The cliff had been formed when an ancient glacier had collided with the hill while the glacier was making it's way downstream. The glacier won the fight, of course, but rather than leaving the smoothly polished surface generally associated with glaciers it had cut into partially decomposed granite that had flaked upon impact, subsequently making the cliff a stairway of miniature steps and a favored practice-scramble for local climbers. Such as was rafting of any of the rivers which came through the heart of town, climbing "The Face" had been made illegal by the Town Council. In a town with a sales-tax-based economy where there weren't enough parking places for the people who wanted to shop and eat, there were certainly not any extra spaces for the people who came just for fun; a line of thought which naturally beckoned every climber who wanted a sinister notch in his ice axe. These dozen climbers knew each other, knew their sport, and knew the face they were about to descend. They'd better know the face they were about to descend because they had all been doing it three times a night for the last several nights. The first night was to map The Wall, to find the most highly visible route which would accommodate what they needed to do. To have three or four climbers on The Wall at a time stretching ropes and calling to each other while breaking the law in the most visible spot in town was madness, considering that for all the joking and name-calling and vile language that accompanied the planning of the project, these people didn't really want to go to jail. So it took two entire nights of scampering up and down, dodging not only the view from the occasional cop but also any wandering Iowan who might spot them and point them out to attention-gathering onlookers. As groundwork for the last night they had stitched little cloth tassels every five feet along the length of hundred-foot climbing ropes then, using the ropes as giant measuring tapes, they placed the flares across the cliff. With letters fifty feet high and fifty feet wide, it took over five-hundred feet of the length of The Face to make the nine-letter message they wrote, and now the only question was when the message would be broadcast.

Some of them thought that the flares should be lit immediately in case anyone on the street were to actually look at The Wall tomorrow and notice hundreds of little red sticks in an untenable place for hundreds of little red sticks. Others disagreed, saying that there was almost nobody around to appreciate it this time of night and it should be saved until dusk the next evening so more people could share and enjoy. What they had in common was they wanted it done and the word had gotten around that it was going down soon. That was good, soon. The fish had been the signal, the sign needed to tell them when to go. Do it and be done with it. If not soon, things could get totally out of control and then the shock element would be down the shitter. Nobody had wanted Low Stakes Gambling in the town to begin with, and that pompous-ass Eddie Swanson was about to find out just how serious the citizens of Estes Park were about getting rid of it.

*   *   *   *   *

It would have been better if the Lake had remained frozen as late this year as it normally does. Gasoline floats on water and that was the whole point of this exercise, but it also would have melted a lot of ice, had there been enough ice to melt, and it isn't too often you get to leave a blackened crater in the middle of a lake.

I wasn't overly worried about getting caught at the Marina if I took a few reasonable precautions. The Recreation Department wouldn't even start looking for their Summer help for another month and that gave them more than enough time during the day to put a

157

few boats in the water and replace a spark plug. They wouldn't be here tonight, and neither, it seemed, would the Police. This time of night at this time of year it's not too common to see a Police Car on the same street you're travelling because there aren't too many cops out to begin with, and the few there are generally park in the shadows behind The Wheel, lurking for locals. Why all six of the patrol cars were in use on a Tuesday night was a mystery to me, and it looked like most of the Police Officers were there too.

It had seemed like a good idea to park PIGIRON in the municipal lot and hoof it for the mile or so to the Marina because while nobody would take much interest in me going there, everybody and his cat would be interested in seeing me leave. That's when I saw the cops. The rear of the Muni, the part that abuts the parking lot, was lit up like a Homecoming Game and all the police cars were parked helter-skelter near the rear door. Maybe the Cop Shop got robbed. I've heard of that happening, when there had been an exceptionally large drug bust and the Police Chief's safe was bulging with goodies, but not here in Estes. They were sure bustling-around about something, though; leaning into the patrol cars to talk on the radios, then getting back out to shout something to the guy by the door or to the men on the roof or in another patrol car. Everybody shouting, engines roaring, headlights glaring and blue-and-red light-bars flashing, it would have made Max Sennet proud to see that his Keystone Kops had come this far. Interesting as it may have been to stick around and watch, I'm going to leave them to make it on their own. I have a date with five gas tanks.

I'd noticed when I was strolling through the Marina a couple days ago that all the valves on the Marina's fuel tanks had padlocks on them, chaining them closed and keeping them safe from harm. Mighty locks that could stay fast under the impact of a high-calibre bullet. Powerful locks that could withstand the ravaging elements. Stupid locks that became irrelevant once I had twisted-out the screw that held the valve's handle in place and discarded the handle with it's lock intact. The small pipe wrench I brought was almost too big for the job.

The hard part had been stretching the Marina's fire hose out into the lake, and I had almost abandoned that idea. There may not be much ice on the lake but that didn't mean the water was warm enough to swim in, and I could barely lift the weight of 150 feet of one-and-a-half-inch hose, much less swim with it if I had wanted to. Fortunately the boys who ran the Marina were getting in a little pre-season fishing, or had been until the dead Trout started floating into the lake from town, and they'd thoughtfully left a rowboat up on shore. Those rusty oarlocks made a terrible noise and the calm surface of the lake did nothing to muffle it, but few people live within earshot of here and those who did were probably trying to get their dogs to stop barking. For some reason, it seemed like every dog in town had started barking, all at once.

The plan was simple enough on paper, but I'm not a Physicist and there was a very good chance that I'd omitted something from the equation. Still, it was worth a try and that's what I'm giving it. Gasoline floats on water; that's a given. What I was hoping was that the head pressure developed by the gasoline being stored thirty feet above the lake's surface would be sufficient to force the gas to flow to the end of the hose on the bottom of the lake where it would then be free to bubble to the surface well away from the shore and the buildings of the Marina. I don't have any problem with the guys who run the Marina. They're a couple of ski-bums who climb the rocks around Estes in the Summer and wander over to Vail or Steamboat for the rest of the year, and would more than likely take some sort of perverse delight in what I was doing if I weren't doing it with their gasoline.

The rest of it was almost too simple. The one-inch pipe from the final tank in the series, the pipe which led to the gas pump on the dock, had been left above ground so that if it developed any leaks they wouldn't be a secret. Whomever designed the less-than-sophisticated plumbing required to get the gasoline from the tanks to the pump had come to the realization that, by needing to thread one end of the pipe into the valve at the last tank and needing to thread the other end into the pump, it would be necessary to cleverly install a union smack-dab in the middle of the fifty-foot run, and that union came apart easily. Once I had cut the fitting from one end of the fire hose, slipped it over the now-open union and clamped it in place, all there was to do was to open the valve and let gravity do the rest. Not yet, though. Wait until the moment was right. Wait until I built the nerve to do it, too. So far I've been angry and moving on adrenalin, but now that the moment of truth had arrived I could feel the butterflies. Not that I'd ever had any doubts that the deed would get done, but now was the time to sit down and take a deep breath and be calm for a moment. Hell, I'm a Waiter, not a terrorist, and the worst thing that could happen to me, short of getting caught, would be that I could never tell anybody that I was the person who had done it. Tony would know, though, and that's who I'm doing it for. When the dead Trout had eventually found their way to the mouth of the lake the City Fathers could have made at least a little effort to keep them out. A Volleyball net would have almost done it, but evidently even that was too much to ask of them. Now the Lake smelled as bad as the Town, the rotting and bloated corpses of the hundreds of dead fish poisoning the water almost guaranteed a major lapse in the visitor-count next season. I hadn't killed all those fish with polluting the Lake in mind; when I killed all those fish the only thing on my mind was avenging Tony, and the ironic thing was that Tony didn't fish.

*   *   *   *   *

The reopening of the Oliver Hotel had been rumored for some time, but in Estes Park everything and everyone gets a turn in the rumor mill, so until the trucks began to arrive with materials and the local contractors began scampering for local help, the event was taken as only gossip. The first sign was when one long-haired, scraggly-bearded, lanky roofer, one of the original of The Rev. Simms' flock, began spending a lot of time crawling around the eaves of The Hotel taking measurements and writing down figures: "Andor The Barbarian" was dragging a ruler across the roof.

Their combined grins would have made the Cheshire Cat blush. "The Hardy Group" was the name they had selected for the company they had established to administer The Oliver Hotel, a name chosen partly as a reflection of their sense of humor and partly because of what they had endured to get this far, and when "The Group" was formed the objectives had been very specific and almost too simple to be valid. "What do you do with three floors of rooms, a three hundred fifty seat restaurant with an attendant kitchen, and a seventy five seat bar? Two of the three floors of would go to the

160

people who are footing the bill, the guests, but that kitchen, John, do you realize it's potential?"

"If you can get the right people to drive it. The biggest gripe I've heard about this place was the food."

"The biggest gripe I've heard about The Hotel has been The Hotel, which is presumably why it went back to The IRS."

"Look, Antoine, the last people to own The Oliver Hotel acted like they wanted it as a tax write-off, but there were a number of owners before them who genuinely tried to make it work and failed. What's your 'Ace in the hole', what do you know that they don't?"

"The 'Ace in the hole', as you put it, is the entire forth floor. The rooms on that floor were built to house the servants of the people who originally stayed here and were never meant to actually be a part of The Hotel, and when you over-charge a guest to trudge his luggage up three flights of stairs and give him a dingy room, that will be his memory of his stay. Those rooms will be closed from the guests of The Hotel and I hope that at least one bad memory will be closed with them."

"By turning a four story hotel into a three story hotel, you can turn a profit?"

"It can help prevent a loss. Besides, I have other plans for those rooms. Do you remember Judy, the member of my Parish who did all that baking of bread and stuff? Do you know where she learned her craft?"

"I figured she just did it, that it was something she'd just picked up, but, yes, I do remember her. I remember those toasty sweet rolls she'd bring by on a freezing cold morning even better."

"She was a baking instructor in a culinary institute until one morning she woke up and realized that she couldn't stand living in the city any longer."

"A lot of us got here that way."

"And a lot of us can't make a year-round living once we get here, but what if I could find a half-dozen more people like Judy, people with genuine skills in the Culinary Arts? All that space in the basement that was used for sales offices could easily be turned into classrooms and the empty rooms on the forth floor could become student housing. John, there isn't a valid Culinary School within a thousand miles of here, and we've just had one put in our lap."

"That should take care of any potential complaints about the food, I guess."

"You guess? You 'guess' that we could guarantee the finest food on the Front Range, or at least the best in this town, which is where our patrons happen to be when they get hungry."

"And how much do you think this is going to cost?"

"To install initially, I'm guessing about three pints of gold. To maintain on an annual basis, there's a pint of gold per year set aside for the first five years. If it still needs outside support after that I'm doing it wrong."

"So you can look to a gallon of gold just to fix-up your fuck-ups?"

"I don't anticipate 'fuck-ups', John, or I wouldn't have started this venture in the first place. Hedging against unforeseen contingencies, if we do it right it, we won't need that gold. If I have my head up my ass, the extra gold will allow us enough room to recognize that we have made an obvious mistake and clean it up."

"Not that I don't like the idea, but what do you know about running a school?"

"Not squat, my friend, not squat. That's the beauty of it.

"Well put and noble. How are you going to run a school?"

"What I plan, what I have envisioned from the onset, is to have the entire establishment run by the students."

"Antoine, what you're looking for is to have people educate themselves and pay you for the privilege of doing it. It reeks of a sleazy scam."

"There's nothing sleazy about it. Any student is going to teach himself. It matters how the information is disseminated and it matters what is demanded by the school, but it is ultimately up to the student to do the learning, to teach himself. We get the best instructors and set the finest curriculum, and the students' contribution to The Hotel would ensure that the tuition could be kept low enough to make the school easily affordable."

"A company-store labor camp?"

"Point taken. Now, where was I?"

"Pontificating."

"Oh, yeah. Anyway, combine that with The Hotel being run by people who really want to make The Hotel successful, John, I don't see how it can fail."

"I do, and it can fail real fast. What's to stop every hotel and restaurant in town from calling itself a school and charging people to work there?"

"Nothing is stopping them. Not now nor in the past. But running a school isn't easy and it's not always fun. It takes a lot of dedication to make a school work, and more than just a little talent on your side to become accredited with the State. We have something else on our side, too, and that's affordable housing. The entire forth floor could be dedicated to quarters for the students; the Institute's, mine, and yours."

"Mine? I'm not planning on doing any teaching."

"What do you call what you've been doing all Winter? You are every bit as enthusiastic about spreading the word of Native American Law as I am about spreading the word of God. Which brings us back to the forth floor; it wouldn't hurt my feelings to cache a Religious Retreat up there somewhere, too."

"You're really into this, aren't you?"

"Was there ever any question?"

"It never hurts to ask."

"In other words, you're a superstitious man."

"Yeah."

"So am I. Perhaps that's why I'm a free-lance Preacher."

*   *   *   *   *

Some people like the smell of gasoline, but I'm not one of them. I don't find it repulsive in-and-of itself, but it smells like a dangerous situation and I don't like dangerous situations, especially when I'm not in control. Nobody is in control of gasoline fumes. Nobody. The only control over gasoline fumes is to not allow them to exist, to keep the cap on the can, and I hadn't kept the cap on the can tonight for damned sure.

The fumes I had been smelling for the last half hour had been the ones from my shoes, from when I'd broken the union-joint open and spilled the gas that had been in the pipe onto them. The pipe hadn't been full by any measure because those rock-climbing, slope-scraping, wandering gypsies did a damn fine job of draining tanks and lines against a Winter of valve-seeping attrition, but they weren't set up to handle five months of full tanks and eventually a little of the gas had leaked passed the valve. The shoes were pre-destined to become sacrificial lambs from the on-set of this adventure anyway because I knew I'd be leaving lots of footprints and I didn't want to become Cinderella once the investigation got underway, but right now as the gasoline was evaporating they were certainly making my feet cold. That could have nudged me into action a little earlier than I would have otherwise been moved, but it was the blaring of the Volunteer Fire Department's siren that woke me up. Climbing out of the little pocket where I'd hidden myself, I could easily see what the commotion was about; the whole side of the cliff, the one on the South side of the shopping district, the entire cliff was on fire. Bright, intense, yellow-white fire, it almost seemed to be spelling something. I couldn't be sure from this distance, but I have a job of my own to do now. If one fire was good, then two fires should be great.

When I first opened the valve the gasoline began to flow beautifully, but then it just stopped. Shit! I'd dropped one end of the firehose way out into the lake and then once I was back on shore I'd dragged the other end thirty feet back to the exposed end of the gas pipe just to make sure there weren't any kinks in the line, and now the gas had stopped flowing anyway. Shit and damn! This had gone too smoothly to have it go sour now. Then it struck me, like when you find yourself trying to change channels on the TV with the remote control for the VCR. Of course the gasoline had stopped flowing; there was nothing to displace the gasoline inside the tanks and it was pulling a vacuum on itself, so naturally it had stopped flowing. Even before the vent plug on the uppermost tank was completely loose I could hear air being sucked passed it, and once it was out of it's hole the noise made by the air roaring in sounded a little like a jet airplane and a lot like too loud. This was it; this was party time, and already the fumes from the gasoline rising to the surface of the lake were becoming nauseatingly thick.

The weakest link in this chain of disaster had been how to ignite the mess once I had made it, and to this end I decided on using highway flares. They're pretty much waterproof and sure make a hot flame, but it hadn't been possible for me to test the idea until now. I needn't have worried my little self about that at all.

I brought a surprisingly-difficult-to-purchase package of three flares with me just in case I didn't get it on the first try, but one of them proved ample. The flare had hardly crested the arc of it's trajectory after I'd flung it with all my might when the air around it began glowing with a bright blue light. As the flare dropped toward the water the light got bigger and bigger and brighter and brighter until it exploded with a force that almost knocked me down; like somebody had just thrown a wet mattress on me, a hot, wet mattress. It was incredible. The ball of fire in the air ignited the pool of gasoline on the lake's surface, and it erupted with a geyser of flame that formed a mushroom cloud that approached a hundred feet in height. My God, what have I done?

Time to boogie my frail ass out of here, beat feet, hasten my adieu! My shoes came off as soon as I got to the asphalt parking lot, and that's just where I left them because between the gasoline that had soaked through them and the wiping clean of any fingerprints I had done before this stunt had begun I wasn't too worried of having them traced back to me. My plan had been to waddle down the highway for a while before taking to the woods in order not to make any more footprints in the area, but the fire was raging mightily and the night had become too bright for me to chance being seen so I cut straight across the road and into the cover of the trees. Just in time, too, for the first of a growing line of cars was beginning to slow down to have a look. The flashlight I brought with me was a little weenie flashlight that allowed me to see something close and still not emit enough light to be visible for a great distance, which was a good idea for the job but made trotting back to town a bit treacherous. The ground was basically level, but wherever an Elk had stepped when the ground was wet and thawed made a lovely opportunity for a twisted ankle. With that, I hardly travelled faster than a brisk walk back to PIGIRON, but I had the fire on the lake to keep me company and the fire on the cliff to watch, and that fire on the cliff did spell something, and it became more and more clear as I approached town until finally the words came into focus:

FUCK EDDIE

it read, and it read it loud and clear.

* * * * *

"I'd like to see Eddie Swanson". Paulli wasn't being rude, but he obviously wasn't into playing games. He had been up most of the night.

"I'm sorry, Sir, but Mr. Swanson is quite busy at the moment and unavailable to see anyone. If you'd care to ..."

"I'd care to see Eddie Swanson, and I don't give a damn about his agenda, although thank you for asking". With that, Pauli strode toward the door. Eddie's office was in a public building and the warrant Pauli carried for his arrest was also a warrant to enter. Neither would the two young FBI Agents he'd brought with him be denied access. This was going to be their bust, something to give them a little confidence, and they were going to be graded on it. Eddie Swanson had just become a 'Pop Quiz'.

Pauli and the Agents had met for dinner with the Mayor and his wife several nights ago, at the Mayor's request. Pauli had introduced himself to Frank Parker earlier that day in a prearranged meeting on the job site of Parker's latest project and had explained in detail what he wanted to do. In a statement to the newspaper explaining why he wasn't going to seek reelection to another term, Frank Parker hadn't used the word 'corruption', but he didn't stray too far from it, either, and that had given Pauli confidence that he was a man to be trusted.

"Frank," (the two men had hit-it-off immediately and dispensed with all formalities) "the IRS has been hinting about an interest in the financial dealings of Estes Park and would very much like to take a can opener to the ledgers. What they don't want to do is create a big stink just before the tourist season starts".

166

"That seems to be more thoughtful than they are usually given credit for being."

"The difference between the IRS and any other Federal Bureaucracy is the direction of the flow of money through it, and anybody who is taking money instead of giving money is automatically the bad guy. They aren't without feelings, it's just that they don't often get the opportunity to display them."

"Well, I appreciate the thought, but it really won't be necessary for them to do anything because it's already been done."

"We've known for some time that something stinky has been going on", Elaine Parker added. "So for the last two months Frank has been doing something about it." Her obvious pride in her husband was apparent.

"Our son is an Accountant", Frank said. "With their daughter in college, he and his wife semi-retired for an extended vacation and spent Christmas with us. It was so nice to have 'young people' in the house again that we convinced them to stick around for awhile. I'd told him about my suspicions and he audited the books for me, one at a time in my office, and the Town never knew it."

"And he found ...?"

"He found. I don't know how much he missed, but he found enough to nail Eddie Swanson on a number of things, and unpaid taxes seems to be just the beginning. That's what should interest you the most."

"It's certainly a place to start. Do you have any documentation?"

"Tons of it. I just haven't known who to give it to, yet. You see, I don't like Swanson even a little bit. He's a treacherous, pompous ass, and he's been using this town for his personal gain for too many years. The other side of the coin is that while he's taken a lot from the town, he's given back even more. That's what he gets paid to do, I know, but I think it might be difficult to find anybody with his insight to replace him."

"Everybody is replaceable. Ask Richard Nixon. When do I get to see the paperwork?"

"Right now." Elaine Parker removed an over-stuffed manila envelope from her huge purse and handed it across the table. "That's enough to get you started, Pauli," she said. "We've got two

167

boxes filled with photocopies of the town's financial records going back fifteen years, along with a sworn affidavit from our son. He's very thorough, you know."

Pauli paid for the dinner and left a tip that reflected his mood. Now it was time for his 'boys' to do their job.

The three men had almost reached Eddie Swanson's door when Pauli stopped abruptly and turned to glance back at the Secretary. As he had suspected, she had lifted the telephone handset off it's cradle and was punching buttons when Pauli caught her eye with a crooked smile, at which time she weakly smiled back at him then simply shrugged and put the phone back in it's cradle. More as a courtesy than anything else, Pauli had the Junior G-Men knock on the door before they entered, and then had them identify themselves both verbally and with their Identification Cards once they were face-to-face with Swanson. And he had insisted that they be courteous.

"Above all, be courteous", Pauli had reminded them. "If you go in there and be rude it will have two effects. First, it will make you a bully in the eyes of the person you're arresting. That will make him react in one of three ways. He'll become enraged and strike out at you, or he'll become insulted and despise you, or he'll cower in fear. Of the three, having him cower is the worst thing that can happen because at that point he has the capacity to change personalities unpredictably, literally go insane. You have the law and you have the Badges and you have the guns and you don't need the attitude. That's the second effect being rude will have on you. You get an 'attitude' and you get a world of shit. You think you're Superman, you think that every Civilian is a turd, and you may even get to enjoy it. Any one of those things can make you very dead very fast, so don't be rude. Too many variables. You don't need those variables in your life because if it comes down to it you'll ultimately be backed up by the U.S. Army. Don't be rude because you don't need to rude in order to be correct. It doesn't pay. Questions? Okay, do the best you can and I'll just watch."

And watch them he did. He watched them enter the office, he watched them almost stumble on their lines, and he watched them duck-and-cover as Eddie Swanson picked the large rock up over his head and hurl it at them. Eddie had been standing by The Rock when they had entered his office, calmly stroking the vein of quartz with the thumb of his right hand and caressing the side with his left. Giving a 'hand job' to a piece of stone was a new one to Pauli, although his ex-wife might have said that she'd been doing it for years.

He could critique 'the boys' later. They'd graduated from The Academy with honors and were capable of doing their job. They were also capable of being intimidated by a stocky middle-aged cop who knew the ropes, one who had 'been there', one who was grading them on their performance. Pauli would cut them some slack where he need to cut them slack, whether they knew it or not. There's never any reason to be rude.

Pauli took two giant steps toward Swanson, pivoting on his right leg and landing with his left leg just behind Eddie's feet. With a sweeping motion and twisting his body to the right, Pauli's left hand slammed into the man's chest and walloped him onto his back. Karate has it's benefits, Pauli always thought to himself during moments such as this, but brute force and awkwardness also have a place in the greater scheme of things. It's probably a lot the same thing but with different techniques. Almost automatically Pauli's .357 was lodged under Eddie's nose, pinning him to the floor roughly as hard as Pauli's left knee on Eddies sternum was restricting his breathing.

"You're under arrest, of course, but from your actions you seemed to have been contemplating that when we came in." Pauli's voice could barely be heard across the room. "Why would you think anyone would want to arrest you? You've been naughty, haven't you, Eddie? That's why you think someone would want to arrest you, isn't it? Gentlemen," he said, more audibly this time, "would one of you please read this man his 'Rights' while the other of you is clearing the room? Thank you." The noise made by The Rock smashing the wall's panelling and then crashing to the floor hadn't gone unnoticed, and the office had begun to fill with the morbidly curious.

The last of the gawkers had reluctantly backed out of the door after stealing one last glance at the man who evidently wasn't going to be their boss much longer when a Uniformed Policeman pushed his way passed them and into the room.

"What's going on here?" he bellowed, putting his hand on his gun.

"FBI", said the Agent standing closest to him while he produced his ID with one hand and immobilized the cop's trigger finger with the other. "This man is our prisoner."

"The Hell he is!", the cop shouted as he spun toward the Agent, bringing with him a round-house-left aimed at eye-level.

The Agent nimbly ducked the blow and, still holding the immobilized trigger finger, brought his other hand behind the still-swinging elbow and drove it into the wall at the same time he sprang up behind his adversary and pushed his shoulder into the cop's spine. Had he been listening for it, Pauli thought later, he would have liked to have counted the breaks, the bones snapping and the joints being ripped from their sockets. He thought maybe three, but it could have been only two long ones or even as many as five simultaneous breaks. Whatever it was, the boy had some moves of his own, Pauli smiled to himself.

"Officer," the second Agent politely said, "you are under arrest for the obstruction of justice and attacking a Federal Agent after he had duly identified himself. You will now be handcuffed and disarmed, and should you choose to resist I will use the force required to stop you."

He was holding his piece in the correct manner, Pauli noted. The hammer was back and both of his hands on the Pachmyer grips were steady. Good Lad, but it wasn't necessary. The cop had "gone down on himself" and become a snivelling heap on the floor with both of the elbows on his left arm going in different directions as they pointed to his now-restrained wrists.

"Uncle Ed," the Policeman slobbered. "make them stop!"

Uncle Ed?

"Shut up, Rupert! I don't need your help and you're not getting any more of mine."

"Rupert?", Pauli thought to himself. Nobody's really named Rupert. Jimmy was right; Buford fit him a lot better. And that's when Pauli made a stupid mistake: He allowed a relaxed moment while he shut his eyes and softly laughed to himself. That's what gave Eddie Swanson the chance to spit in Pauli's face. Not in his face, actually, because the revolver barrel compressing his upper lip denied Swanson a true aim. What the revolver barrel did next was to plug the hole from where the spit originated.

A person doesn't have the luxury of deciding how fast to pull a trigger once the decision to pull it has been made. Something like that can be equated to the immortality of youth.

*   *   *   *   *

"And you knew they found the gold at The Hotel?"

"Yup."

"Your gold? And you're not going to tell anybody?"

"Yup, and nope."

"What about unpaid taxes or something like that? Those seem to be a big motivator of legal action in town these days."

"Jimmy, life begins when you start minding your own business."

It was obvious that Spring was approaching. The Eagles and Ravens, the two birds that make themselves most obvious during the winter, were slowly being displaced by the smaller seasonal occupants, the "Snow Birds", who were soon to be joined by their larger seasonal occupants, the "Snow Birds". And the tourists were on their way back, too. They weren't here in the hoards of summer yet, but we could see the whites of their headlights carving the canyon on their way into town. The Wheel Bar hadn't yet reached capacity either, but even at this time of night Pauli and I had found it more comfortable sitting at one of the miniature tables than at the bar, he with his Black Jack/Rocks and me with a Bud and a taste of Jim Beam.

"What I don't understand", Pauli continued, "is why the FBI dropped that training program. It was a great idea that seemed to be working as well as any program could be expected to do in it's first few months."

"Maybe they were afraid they couldn't live up to their old reputation."

"You don't really think that, Jimmy."

"No, I don't. I don't have the slightest idea how much trouble it is to have a new Federal program funded, but I've got to believe it's a major pain in the ass."

171

"At least that. I don't even want to guess what it cost them to have me and another dozen guys just like me from around the country doing this, and to shut it down overnight meant that every tax dollar spent should have been thrown down the toilet at the onset with no questions asked and thereby saving everybody else a lot of time and trouble."

"Face it, Pauli, you're an aging warrior and your leaders are rewarding you as they have always rewarded aging warriors of a dying cause, and that is by forgetting them. You've aligned yourself with losers who ask too little of you."

"Jesus H. Christ, Jimmy! I have a basic Goddamned belief in my Country and the same belief that the system is good and can work!" His face was flushed in anger as he inhaled the last of his drink. "That's all I have or need to say. Other than what do you think will happen with the Low Stakes Gambling Law?"

"Ain't shit happening with any gambling in this town and these are on me." Marlin had suddenly materialized in his own special way with three glasses balanced in one hand as he picked-up the empties with the other. "I hear that the 'Vegas people withdrew their offer."

"Maybe looks like you got a clean slate, Jimmy, so why are you crying?"

"I'm not crying", I sniffed, dragging the bandana out of my right-rear pocket and wiping it under my nose. "I have nothing to cry for. This isn't my town. I've been doing nothing more for the last eleven years than passing through, and if I've made a living and some friends and a few loose ties, well, I've never had a problem making friends and this town doesn't need to be an exception."

"Then what are you running from?"

"Maybe somebody who asks too many questions. Pauli, I'm tired and want to go to bed. Maybe I'll catch you the next time you're in town." With that I walked out of The Wheel Bar, hoping that at this time of night I wouldn't get hassled by the cops because I'm a local.

The Author was raised on the Southern
California Coast, did two tours in Viet Nam,
earned an MBA from Portland State
University, and then went prospecting for
three and a half years.
He came to Estes Park by accident in 1984
and basically never went away. He is not
married, is not gay, and has never lived in
New York City.